A Coal Miner's Bride

The Diary of Anetka Kaminska

by Susan Campbell Bartoletti

Scholastic Inc. New York

Sadowka, Poland
1896

Thursday, April 16, 1896

This morning I scraped the hairy backs of our pigs and collected a good crop of long, black bristles. I sold them to Mr. Levy, the cobbler. He uses the bristles to sew boots and shoes.

How we haggled over the price! I asked high. Mr. Levy offered low. I argued. He argued back. I waved my arms. He waved his. I paced. He paced. I knew I would win, for our pigs have the finest bristles, and besides, Mr. Levy likes my spirit, I can tell.

In the end, we were both satisfied, I with my coins and he with his bristles. I wrapped the coins in my handkerchief and dropped it into my apron pocket. I wished him many customers, and he wished me "Shalom."

As I left the cobbler shop, I saw three soldiers standing across the street. It angers me to see soldiers parading about in Russian uniforms, especially because many are Polish boys, forced to serve in the Czar's army.

I pulled my kerchief over my head and started down the stone street, past the weaver and tailor shops, the marketplace, the mayor's and clerk's offices, and the jail. I took care not to touch my pocket, for Mamusia always warned me that's a sure way of telling others I am carrying something important.

Just outside the village, where the stone street turns to dirt, I met a Gypsy woman with her husband. The husband was hitched to a heaped cart, covered with a moth-eaten, red-and-yellow woolen blanket. His horse — a gray, swaybacked mare — was tethered behind the cart, strolling as nice as you please.

"I know I should put the horse before the cart," said the husband good-naturedly. He mopped his forehead with his shirtsleeve. "But she turned up lame this morning and has taken the day off."

His wife had white hair like Babcia, but her face was smooth and beautiful. "What would you like to buy today?" she asked. She yanked the blanket from the cart. Oh, what a heap of pots, pans, and kettles; necklaces and religious charms; bundles of colorful ribbons and lace; newspapers and books.

Books! My heart leaped, but then I saw they were Russian. The Czar seems determined to ban everything Polish — from our language, to our national dress, to our dances, to our songs.

I reached for a plain black book with no fancy gold letters on its spine. I opened the cover, so new the binding crackled. The pages were blank. An empty book! A book that could be anything I wanted it to be! I got it in my head that I would like to fill the pages with my own private thoughts, Polish thoughts.

The coins felt heavy in my pocket. I knew Babcia needed them to pay our taxes, but oh, I wanted that book. "How much?" I asked, trying not to sound eager.

"An empty book cannot help a girl catch a suitor," said the Gypsy woman. "Surely you would prefer ribbons or lace for your hair?"

"The book," I said again. "How much?"

The Gypsy touched my face. "You're a pretty girl," she said. "What husband wants a wife who knows more than he does?" She looked at her husband and sighed in a woeful manner.

I dug in my pocket for the coins and dropped them all into her hand. "I will pay this for the book — and for two ribbons."

"You drive a hard bargain," she moaned.

It wasn't a hard bargain, but fair enough. Now I have two pretty ribbons, one yellow, one purple, and a book of my own in which to set down my days.

Friday, April 17, 1896

Babcia scolded me for wasting the coins on this book. Now I feel terribly selfish, as if I have stolen bread from the mouths of my brother and grandmother. "I'm sorry," I told her. "The bristles did not belong to me."

"Anetka," she said, "what good is an empty book?"

How could I explain the hope and promise that something so empty holds? "Everyone has something to say," I told her. "And I want to say it in Polish, no matter what laws the Czar makes."

Babcia's wrinkled face softened. *"Masz hart ducha,"* she said, thumping her chest. "You have a spirited heart, just like your mother. I will tell the pigs to hurry up and sprout more bristles."

I liked hearing that I have Mamusia's spirit. I kissed my grandmother's cheek and promised not to be reckless again. From now on, I will guard each coin.

SUNDAY, APRIL 19, 1896

Last night the oldest Jablonski boy knocked on the door. He is Jozef's age, seven. "Our cow is having trouble with her calf," he said. "Can you come?" My grandmother is famous throughout the village for her veterinary skill, and some day I will be, too.

We hurried to the Jablonski cottage, five cottages and one field from us. The Jablonskis have three children, not counting the littlest girl, who died last winter before she turned a year old. If that wasn't sorrowful enough, their cottage caught fire in the spring. Babcia says trouble always comes in threes.

The cow lay on a bed of straw, too weak to pick up her head. She had been laboring for several hours. Babcia understood the problem at once. "The calf needs to be turned," she said. "But first we must hobble the mother."

Babcia and I tied a rope around the cow's front and back legs so she would not kick. Babcia is old and tiny, but brave and strong! She rolled up her sleeve, then knelt by the cow's back end and stuck her right arm up to her shoulder into the cow's hind parts. How the cow complained!

Babcia grunted and worked to turn the calf inside. "There," she said at last, withdrawing her arm. We untied the cow and waited. Her sides heaved sharply, as if she were taking a deep breath. Water gushed from her hind parts, then a small nose and head showed in a milky sac. A few more heaves, then shoulders and forelegs appeared, and finally a bloody but brand-new calf slid out. There was a sigh of relief all around.

The cow forgot all her complaints. Eager to greet her new daughter, she curled her big lips back, sniffed her calf all over, then began to clean her with her tongue. Soon the calf climbed to her feet and stood, wobbly, next to her mother. She found her mother's milk bag, and the mother cow made contented, soft lowing noises as her daughter suckled. The Jablonskis paid Babcia with two sacks of rye meal.

On the way home, I told Babcia that if I were that cow, I'd never forget my complaints. The next time the bull talked sweet to me, I would sour him fast. Babcia told me that God intended for labor pain to awaken mother love.

MONDAY, APRIL 20, 1896

Wash day. Babcia and I made starch from rye meal. My hands are red and sore from the hot lye water. I soaked and scrubbed, wrung and rinsed. Jozef refused to help. At seven, he is strong enough, but he fusses about "girl's work."

From our yard, the fields ribbon up the hillside, and I can see the manor house. It belongs to Count Sadowski and sits on top of the hill, overlooking his apple orchard, the village and its whitewashed cottages, willow hedges, and picket fences.

But even a grand manor house has wash day. I could see the Sadowskis' fine bed linen fluttering on the clothesline. I counted ten blouses, ten chemises, and ten skirts, yellows and blues and greens, flapping like the wings of huge, colorful birds.

"I wish I had clothes enough to change every day," I

told Babcia. "All different colors, too — bright yellows and purples and blues and reds."

"Too much wash," she said. "What would you do with so many clothes? You only have one body."

I don't ever want to be practical like my grandmother.

TUESDAY, APRIL 21, 1896

Some people say the farmer is his own boss. They are wrong. We have four bosses: spring, summer, fall, and winter. Right now the spring boss is here. I can tell because the storks have returned to the rooftops and the pussy willows are changing color. I have also counted three thunderstorms. Babcia says it takes three thunderstorms to herald spring's arrival.

Tata doesn't like such fickle bosses. So after Mamusia died, he went to America, where he works in a Pennsylvania coal mine. He has been gone nearly a year now. Tata says there is so much work in America that a man can pick the work he wants to do. In each letter, he promises to come home as soon as he has saved enough money for my dowry and to pay our taxes.

If there is so much work in America, why hasn't Tata come home yet, his pockets filled with rubles and gold and silver ducats? Never mind! I know the answer. It is not the land's fault we are poor. Tata has never had a head for farming or for money. It was always Mamusia who managed the family purse and haggled over the best price for our grain.

I am like Mamusia. I am grateful for the spring boss. The plowing and harrowing are done. Soon the flowers and plants will push through the earth, and the meadows, gardens, and woods will fill with humming bees. Last year I collected a good crop of honey and beeswax to sell. I hope to collect a good crop again.

WEDNESDAY, APRIL 22, 1896

Bread baked. Ten loaves sit cooling on the table. I like Wednesdays best, after the baking is done, when the boys and girls come to our cottage for weekly lessons. I enjoy teaching them to read and write Polish, the way Mamusia did before she died. As a little girl, Mamusia learned from the Countess Sadowska herself. Babcia cannot read and won't let me teach her. Stubborn.

I wish the children could learn Polish in the village school, but since the Czar has banned Polish, the lessons are taught in Russian. The Polish language is forbidden even at playtime. One boy was shut up in a dark closet for twenty-four hours because he spoke to his friend in Polish during playtime. In Pikulka, a young woman was ordered to stop teaching, and when she didn't, soldiers arrested her and took her far away. Babcia says Siberia. Anyone or anything that betrays a love for Polish is forbidden.

The children and I are careful. If we hear someone coming, the girls hide their slates beneath their sewing, and the boys slip theirs beneath their shirts.

FRIDAY, APRIL 24, 1896

I cleaned out my wooden bee boxes this morning. The boxes are ready for bees, and so am I.

MONDAY, APRIL 27, 1896

It is late, after the rooster's first crow. My fingers are shaking as I write this by the light of a pine-knot torch.

Tonight we were awakened by a commotion and the smell of smoke. Jozef, Babcia, and I ran outside in our nightshirts. At the far end of the village, we saw flames and smoke. My heart stopped with dread for my friend Mr. Levy and his family.

"What is it?" Jozef asked, his eyes wide.

"A demonstration," I told him. That's what the Russian soldiers call it when they plunder the homes and shops of Jewish people. I know it happens in other villages, but I didn't think it could happen in Sadowka. How can people be so cruel? I pray that the Levys and the other Jewish families are safe.

TUESDAY, APRIL 28, 1896

Mr. Levy's shop is ruined. Windows are smashed, his workbench broken, and all his shoes and boots are gone. He and his family are badly shaken, but no one is hurt. Someone had warned the Jewish families, giving them enough time to run into the woods and hide.

I helped the Levys and their friends pack the few belongings they managed to salvage. They say they are leaving Sadowka, maybe even going to America. I will miss the Levys. In America, Mr. Levy says there is no Czar and no Czar's army. In America, a man can vote for his government and send his children to school. In America, a man and his family can be Jewish. Mr. Levy sounds full of America fever, just like Tata's letters.

Near the shop I saw four men. They were talking in low and earnest voices. I heard snatches of their conversation:

"It's too bad about the Jews."

"Too bad, you say? What about us? Why, we can't live because of them."

"They have overrun us here."

"Every shopkeeper is a Jew."

"Poland has tolerated them when no one else would."

"Poland? What Poland? There is no Poland anymore."

"Poland or no Poland, let the Jews live someplace else."

I felt shame at hearing my own countrymen talk that way. The talk sounds the same day after day, always going from the problem of the Jews owning the shops to the problem of Poland being divided and ruled by Russia, Austria, and Germany.

I put my head down and started to walk. The more I thought about the Levys and their friends, the angrier I felt. Why shouldn't the Jews own the shops? They aren't allowed to own the land. What else can they do?

How could the Russian soldiers be so heartless? Some are husbands and fathers, just like Mr. Levy. All of them have mothers and fathers. My thoughts grew more jumbled. I turned the corner near the mayor's office and collided with a man.

He was a young soldier, probably not more than eighteen or nineteen years old, judging from his smooth face. He wore a long gray coat, tall black boots, and a cap without a visor. A sabre hung at his side, but neither his uniform nor his sabre mattered to me. As Mamusia would say, I am not a fiery redhead for nothing. I pointed toward the ruined shops. "Tell me," I blurted in my very bad Russian, "are all soldiers born without hearts?"

Amusement flickered in his eyes, clear blue eyes that took in everything like an eagle's. I could tell he wasn't used to having a girl speak to him so directly. "What is your name?" he asked in perfect Russian.

"Anetka," I told him. "Anetka Kaminska."

He looked toward the ruined shops, then back at me, his eyes serious now. "Well, Anetka Kaminska," he said, in Polish this time, "if you knew me, you would know that I am not against the Jews." His Polish sounded crisp, polite but firm.

"Your uniform says otherwise," I said, still in Russian.

He grinned, amused at my boldness. I walked away as he called out in Polish, "*Nazywam się* Leon. My name is Leon Nasevich." I pretended not to hear. I have no desire to know Leon Nasevich or any other soldier.

WEDNESDAY, APRIL 29, 1896

Of all the children, my own brother is the worst to teach. Jozef cannot sit still long enough to learn anything. He squirms and fidgets. If a bird flies past the cottage window, or a cricket chirps, or a toad grunts, his concentration is broken. He'd rather run after the geese or fetch our cow from the meadow.

THURSDAY, APRIL 30, 1896

Yesterday my cat had four kittens. I found them hidden in our small stone grotto for the Virgin Mary. One kitten looks like the orange tom I've seen sneaking about here. Another is black with white feet. Two are smoky gray like their mother. I moved the new little family inside, to the oven corner where it's warm. The mother cat lies there, purring proudly. I hope Babcia lets me keep the black one.

FRIDAY, MAY 1, 1896

May Day. A day of picking flowers and branches to bring new life into the village.

I woke up early to see if I had a maypole erected in the front yard, but nothing. Not even a twig. Last year my best friend, Stefania Krupnik, had two brightly painted spruce poles standing in her yard, which meant two boys liked her. I am not surprised. With her blonde hair and nice smile, Stefania is the prettiest girl in Sadowka. My forehead is too high, my smile too wide, my chin too narrow, my hands and feet too big.

When we were younger, Stefania and I often sneaked away from our work to climb trees or chase each other along the riverbank. Now that we are rounding our thirteenth namesake days, we are too old to do those things.

Our talk has turned to betrothals and marriage and the type of man we hope to marry. We wonder what it is like to be kissed.

This much Stefania and I know already: We don't want an arranged marriage like our mothers and grandmothers and every other woman in the village. We want to marry for love.

SATURDAY, MAY 2, 1896

Bath night. Jozef and I hauled buckets of water from the village well. As I dumped the water into big pots to heat on the stove, Jozef said, "In America, people are so rich that they have pipes to carry the water into the house."

"You sound like Tata," I said. "Full of America fever."

Jozef liked that, I could tell by the proud look that crossed his face. He misses our father.

As the water heated, I dragged the wooden washtub in front of the kitchen stove. I pushed Jozef outside and locked the door. Babcia closed the shutters and gave Jozef a good scolding to keep him from peeking in the windows. My brother is determined to catch me undressed.

Babcia unbraided my hair and brushed it. She loves my hair, which is the same color as Mamusia's, and makes me outstanding in the village. When she was done, I yanked my blouse over my head. Babcia regarded me and said, "You are not a girl anymore, Anetka. You're a young woman, more like sixteen than thirteen. Look how you fill up that old chemise." She went over to the old wooden trunk that holds Mamusia's things and rummaged through it.

I have filled out, which explains why my blouse feels strained across the back and the seams are pulled. I am glad I am getting a figure. I like feeling like a woman, not a girl.

Babcia came back with a blouse and a chemise, so new they were snow white. "Your mother sewed this blouse for you," she said. "She wanted you to dance in it."

I took the blouse from Babcia and fingered the yellow threads of a half-embroidered flower. I haven't danced since Mamusia died from the fever. Babcia said it takes a year of holidays to survive the worst grief. I am better now than I was a year ago, but I still miss my mother terribly. I know Jozef does, too, though he never speaks of her. "I will dance," I promised Babcia. "When Tata comes home, we will all dance."

MONDAY, MAY 4, 1896

The villagers gathered outside the mayor's office today where we waited for our letters. There were men in black jackets and white shirts and ties, the foresters with their guns, peasant men in long coats and muddy boots, women in baggy dresses, and girls in pretty aprons and full skirts.

Stefania waved to me. I went and stood by her. "Maybe you'll get a letter from your father today," she said.

"I hope so," I told her.

Stefania squeezed my hand. "That soldier," she whispered. "He's looking at you."

Private Leon Nasevich stood next to a squinty-eyed sergeant. When our eyes met, Private Nasevich didn't look away but grinned and nodded at me, as if we were old friends. I decided that I didn't like him any more today than the first day we met. He is bold and too sure of himself.

When all the letters were called out, the squinty-eyed sergeant thrust the empty bag at Private Nasevich, then headed across the street to the *gospoda*, the gathering place where men drink vodka. No letter for me.

Stefania sensed my disappointment. "I'm supposed to help my mother take down the wash," she said, "but it's early yet. She won't know if I take the long way home."

Private Nasevich shook the bag. A letter dropped to the ground. He picked it up, stared at it as if he were thinking something over, then stuck it inside his breast pocket.

TUESDAY, MAY 5, 1896

A sunny day. This afternoon Stefania and I visited the Jablonskis' calf. How big she has grown! I told Stefania all about the birth and how Babcia said labor pains awaken mother love. Stefania made a face and said, "I am sure that I can love my babies without labor pains."

WEDNESDAY, MAY 6, 1896

It rained last night, and I awoke with water on my face. Our thatched roof is leaking over our kitchen table and over my mattress. I set out two pots to catch the drips and dragged my mattress to the oven corner so it will dry.

Since it is still raining, I have no choice but to sit inside and sew while Jozef plays with the kittens. I asked Babcia why a girl can do a boy's job, but a boy is seldom expected to do a girl's job. Why do I have to darn Jozef's socks and patch tears in his pants, when he has two hands and ten perfectly good fingers? Babcia told me it is a girl's sacred duty and highest calling to learn to be a good wife and mother.

I look forward to the children coming today for their lessons so I can put away my sewing. With the rain, Jozef will have no excuse to leave!

THURSDAY, MAY 7, 1896

This morning I was up with the sun, squatting on the roof. Most villagers barter with the thatcher, but since we have nothing to trade, it was up to me to replace the disloyal thatch.

I poked and prodded at the reeds, trying to figure out how they fit together. They were tied in thick bundles with grapevine, then tied together again to form long neat rows. It didn't seem much different from sewing a pair of pants. If I can sew, I can surely thatch.

Suddenly, a man's voice greeted me: *"Dzien dobry!"* Startled, I looked down from the roof, into the grinning face of that too-bold, too-sure-of-himself Private Nasevich. "Good day," he said again in Polish, then, "What a strange bird you make. Are you building a nest?"

How dare he call me a bird! "I am thatching a leaking roof," I answered in Polish. "Surely *that* isn't against the Czar's law. Or has yet another law been passed against Polish peasants?"

Private Nasevich looked amused. Then he looked hard at me, and I could tell he was trying not to laugh. "One can hardly tell these days, when there are so many laws," he said. "The Czar forbids everything that he does not know, and I doubt if he knows how to thatch a roof." He shaded his eyes with his hand. "I am impressed that you know."

"I know plenty." I looked him in the eye. "What soldier business brings you here?" I said *soldier* as if it were the dirtiest word, but it didn't seem to bother him.

He took a letter from his pocket. "Business with Anetka Kaminska and her family."

My heart leaped as I recognized Tata's pointy handwriting. Then it struck me: why, it must have been *my* letter that had fallen from the mailbag! At that moment, I knew that Private Nasevich could not be trusted. I climbed down from the roof and held out my hand for the letter.

Teasing me, he held the letter out of my reach and said, "Is that the way you repay someone who has gone to all this trouble?"

O jej! I said to myself. Oh my! I wanted to tell him that all his trouble could have been avoided if he had given me the letter three days ago. But I bit my tongue for fear I might not get Tata's letter at all if I angered him. "What sort of payment?" I asked.

He held the letter as if he were weighing it. "I suppose a letter is worth something to eat."

"Where are your manners, Anetka?" It was Babcia speaking now. She had come from the cow shed and was carrying a pail filled with milk. "Certainly our *guest* can have something to eat." She said *guest* cautiously. Her eyes narrowed, and her chin tilted the way it does when she studies someone.

Cautious Babcia. My grandmother can read a person's character the way some people read books. She won't be fooled by Private Nasevich's polite manner, the way he removes his hat, clicks his heels together and bows politely from the waist. She won't be fooled by his grinning face or his clear blue eyes.

I went inside and cut a thick slice of black bread and cheese and poured a jug of water. Now Private Nasevich is sitting at our kitchen table, eating and talking with Babcia and Jozef while I sit outside waiting for my letter. Jozef is asking question after question about soldier life, and if my nosy brother doesn't shut up, Private Nasevich may never leave, and I may never get Tata's letter.

LATER

I wish I had never met Leon Nasevich. I wish he had never found my letter. I wish he had never delivered it. To devil with him! To devil with that letter! To devil with Tata! To devil! To devil!

AFTER SUPPER

How dare Tata! Does my father think that I belong to him? That I am a table or chair or pair of shoes that he can sell or give away? Has he not noticed that I have flesh and blood? Thoughts and feelings? I hate my father.

BEFORE BED

I still hate my father.

MIDNIGHT, AFTER THE ROOSTER'S FIRST CROW

I cannot sleep. I have taken a candle out to our cow shed and am sitting on a pile of straw as I write this. Babcia would scold me for wasting a candle at this hour, but I fear my heart will burst if I don't write this down.

After Private Nasevich left, I opened Tata's letter. To my surprise, three steamship tickets fell out. Jozef hopped around the kitchen, crowing like a rooster. "Read! Read!" he said. "What does Tata say?"

The words in Tata's letter grip my stomach like a fist. Tata isn't coming home. He wants us to come to America! Tata told me about a coal miner named Mr. Stanley Gawrych who wants a young bride from the old country. So Tata told this Mr. Gawrych that I am young and strong and fit for marriage. I have had good family training and know all I need to take care of a house and a husband. So now Mr. Gawrych has agreed to marry me. Tata promises that we will make a good match. In return, Mr. Gawrych has paid for our passage to America.

"Oh, Babcia," I cried. "How could Tata have done such a terrible thing? I don't want to be a coal miner's bride."

Babcia stroked my hair. "It is a father's duty to find his daughter a good husband."

"To devil with duty!"

Babcia gasped, but I didn't care that I had shocked my grandmother. "Tata promised to come home," I cried. "But now he has traded me for steamship tickets. I don't want to go to America. I don't want to marry a man I do not love."

"What does a young girl know about love?" said Babcia. "My father arranged my marriage, and your grandfather arranged your mother's marriage. This is the way things are done."

I sniffled into my sleeve. "Surely I can do something."

"You can pray," said Babcia. "Pray that you will be a good wife and mother."

Mamusia taught me long ago that if I say my prayers devoutly in Saint Ann's honor, my prayers will be answered, sometimes yes, sometimes no. I will pray. I will pray to Saint Ann, my patron saint. I will pray and watch every day for a sign from her, telling me to disobey my father.

PRAYER TO SAINT ANN

Droga Swieta Anno! Saint Ann, my namesake, my patron saint, Mother of the Blessed Virgin Mary, are you there? Can you hear me? I have not been your most devout daughter, Saint Ann. I have been short-tempered and strong-willed and short of patience. I have been selfish. I don't pray often enough. My mind wanders during Mass. *O Swieta Anno!* I promise to change, if only you will send me a sign that I should not honor my father's wishes.

SUNDAY, MAY 10, 1896

During Mass, I tried to keep my mind on the prayers and sermon, but it kept wandering to stupid tradition.

Babcia says tradition gives our lives order. Without tradition, there would be disorder and confusion. She says a girl cannot know love. She says a girl cannot know how to pick a husband. She says the match is the important thing about marriage. If it is a good match, love will come.

Mass ended without a sign. As I left the church, I saw Private Nasevich sitting alone across the street, reading a book. "How is the village thatcher today?" he called to me. "Or does your roof still leak?"

"My roof doesn't leak," I said.

Babcia looked at me sharply. "It's not a lie," I told her. "Since it has not rained, I don't know if the roof leaks."

I wish I could have thrown a stinging remark at Private Nasevich about the character of a man who sits reading a book when he should be sitting in church.

MONDAY, MAY 11, 1896

Women crowded the well this morning. I spotted Stefania and whispered that I had something important to tell her. I didn't want the other women and girls to overhear. I knew how they would gossip.

The women love to discuss their daughters and potential matches for marriage, to compare the dowries, the number of cows, mares, pigs, and chickens they bring to their marriages, as if the size of a dowry has anything to do with love.

The gossip would be worse for me. The women would cluck their tongues like worried hens and say things like, "*Biedna sierota Anetka!* Poor motherless Anetka, did you know she has no dowry?" or "*Biedna Anetka,* what else can a girl without a dowry do?" or "*Biedna Anetka,* she should count her blessings and consider herself lucky that any man would take her, without a dowry."

Then they would imagine all kinds of stories about Stanley Gawrych, the sort of man who did not ask for a dowry but paid for the passage of his bride. Maybe he's old and fat or ugly and bald with no teeth.

Stefania followed me from the well. We walked until it was safe to talk. I pulled her behind an outbuilding, so nobody could see. "What is it?" asked Stefania.

I burst into tears and told her about Tata's letter. "Oh, you can't go to America," she said. "I will miss you too much." We cried and held each other, and she has promised to pray for a sign, too.

TUESDAY, MAY 12, 1896

No sign. Jozef discovered a Gypsy camp near the woods outside the village. He came home with stories about their dancing and music, and now he says he wants to be a Gypsy. Babcia warned him to stay away from the camp, for the Czar's soldiers don't like Gypsies any more than they like Jews. There is sure to be trouble if the soldiers discover the camp.

WEDNESDAY, MAY 13, 1896

No sign. Babcia is nagging me to sew my wedding sheets.

Thursday, May 14, 1896

Still no sign. It threatened rain all day today but held off until evening. Jozef said he was especially hungry and to please cook extra potato kluski. Sometimes the potato dough gives me trouble and falls apart in the water, but tonight the dumplings boiled just right. I fried them with butter, cabbage, and onions.

Just as we sat down to eat, we heard a knock. Jozef flung open the door, and I was shocked to see Private Nasevich. He was dressed in dark linen pants and a clean white shirt. His face shone as if he had scrubbed it extra hard, and there was a spot of dried blood on his chin where he had cut himself shaving. If I didn't dislike him so much, I would say he looked handsome.

Jozef grinned. "I invited Private Nasevich for supper."

Babcia looked surprised, but she would never turn away a guest. She always says a guest in the home is God in the home. She got an extra bowl and set a place.

My stomach knotted up as I thought of having to eat a meal with Private Nasevich. Yet I have to admit that as much as I dislike him, something about him made me wash my face and tie my new yellow ribbon in my hair.

Jozef asked Private Nasevich question after question about soldier life, barely giving him time to chew between answers. Private Nasevich laughs a lot, a laugh that rolls out from somewhere deep inside him.

After dinner, I cleared away the bowls. Jozef showed off the kittens. "Two males and two females," said Private Nasevich. Jozef wanted to know how he could tell, and Private Nasevich said, "Why, it's stamped on their bottoms."

That made me laugh out loud. Private Nasevich looked pleased that he got me to laugh, which made me cross. Babcia offered him a glass of vodka, but he asked for tea instead. I could tell that pleased my grandmother.

Later I asked Babcia why she treats Private Nasevich so. Babcia said you can tell a lot about a man by the way he laughs. "Laughter," said Babcia. "That's what is missing in Poland."

"Laughter or no laughter, he wears the Czar's uniform," I said.

"He may wear the uniform of a soldier," said Babcia, "but he doesn't wear the heart of one."

Still I have good reason to distrust Private Nasevich's heart, and this is why: The wind picked up outside and it started to rain. To my dismay, he asked if he could wait out the storm.

O jej! My traitorous roof! It rained harder, and I squirmed in agony as a dark patch appeared on the ceiling — right over Private Nasevich's head. Thinking quickly, I suggested that he might be more comfortable near the fire, but he said no, that he was fine. Not a minute later, a drop of rain splashed onto his face. He looked up, saw the dark patch, and held out his hand. Two more drops plopped into it.

"So your roof doesn't leak," he said. He tilted back his head and laughed, a roaring laugh that made me feel foolish and furious at the same time. "You are the most headstrong girl I have ever met."

I knew my face was red because it felt hot, as hot with anger on the outside as I felt on the inside. Private Nasevich has pure, pure meanness in him, and if there is one thing good about America, it's that I will never suffer the displeasure of his company there.

Friday, May 15, 1896

A warm, sunny morning, perfect for hunting bees. From Mamusia I learned to find the hollow tree, the hive hidden high in branches, the place where bees water. The sound of a swarm always thrilled Mamusia. She could hear the bees taking wing, see them become a humming gray cloud, then capture them as they clustered in a tree branch or bush, and bring them home to her wooden bee box.

Once Mamusia told me, "To know bees in your life, you must know bees in your heart." I know bees in my heart, just like my mother.

LATER

Bees buzzed all around me, yet I could not find one hive or one swarm. How could my heart be empty of bees? Was this a sign from Saint Ann? To make matters worse, when I reached our cottage, I saw a strange bird perched on top of our roof. It was Private Nasevich, armed with a bundle of reeds.

"Are you building a nest?" I asked.

"I am thatching your roof," he said, looking quite pleased with himself. "Unless Czar Nicholas has passed a law against patching a leaking roof —"

"You don't have to do that."

"If I don't, who will?"

I was surprised that Jozef hadn't told him. "Nobody will," I blurted out. "Our roof doesn't matter because we are going to America."

"America?" he asked. His grin stiffened.

"My father has sent for us," I said, and I told him about Tata's plan for my marriage.

The grin slid from his face. "And this is what you want?"

"It doesn't matter what I want," I said. "A girl must obey her father," (unless her patron saint intervenes, but I didn't tell him that).

I expected him to tease me about marriage, but he didn't. I suppose a soldier understands duty and obligation.

"Thatch the roof if you like," I told him, "but we have nothing to trade."

"Supper," he said, turning back to the thatching. "You can trade supper for your roof."

Sometimes I think all Private Leon Nasevich cares about is his stomach.

SUNDAY, MAY 17, 1896

It rained hard again last night. Private Nasevich has not even stopped by to see if his thatching worked.

MONDAY, MAY 18, 1896

Still no Private Nasevich. Jozef misses him.

TUESDAY, MAY 19, 1896

I tried to convince Babcia that I won't need wedding sheets since Saint Ann will answer my prayers any day now, but Babcia made me sew them anyway. Then when she examined the stitches, she said, "Not straight enough. Rip them out."

Grumbling, I ripped them out and started over again.

With each stitch I reminded myself how angry I am at Tata and how much I hate his America fever. By afternoon my eyes were tired and sore. Babcia relented and let me hunt for bees. Nothing. Saint Ann! Is this your sign? Are you answering my prayers no?

WEDNESDAY, MAY 20, 1896

Jozef was especially difficult today. All the children showed up for class except for my own brother. In the middle of lessons, the Gypsy woman brought him home, using his ear as a handle.

Her eyes narrowed as she saw the children. She pinched Jozef's ear tighter and said to me, "He was throwing rocks at our rooster. He needs a good switching."

"Let go of his ear," I told her, "and I will see to my brother."

The Gypsy woman left, and I sent the children home. Jozef tried to slide past me, but I collared him. "Why where you throwing rocks at her rooster?" I asked.

"He's a bad rooster," said Jozef. "He was pestering the chickens."

I turned my head so that Jozef wouldn't see me laugh. I don't know if Babcia would approve, but I told him the truth about roosters who pester chickens.

Thursday, May 21, 1896

Usually our rooster crows with great regularity, first at midnight, then at three in the morning, and then at daybreak. But this morning, when we got up at the third crow, it should have been the second crow. We waited a good two hours before the sun rose, because Babcia wouldn't let us be lazy and go back to bed. I was tired and as bad-tempered as bees on a rainy day.

Friday, May 22, 1896

Glupi kogut! Stupid rooster! Again we are up waiting for the sun. Even the cow thought it was too early to let down her milk, so I sat with nothing to do but complain. And another thing: It has been one week since I have seen Private Nasevich. I tell myself his absence is a good sign, yet I know Jozef misses him, so I find myself watching the road for his familiar shape.

Monday, May 25, 1896

Glupi, glupi kogut! If our stupid rooster weren't so scrawny, I would pluck and boil him for dinner.

Tonight Private Nasevich surprised us. He just returned from Warsaw. I noticed that a few hairs had sprouted above his lip. He is trying to grow a mustache. He showed off a clock he had bought.

"You must think yourself quite a person to own a clock," I told him. "Too good for the rooster."

"Anetka," he said, "it's a wedding present for you. Don't you know that every married couple in America owns a clock?"

I am getting too good at stinging remarks for my own good. I noticed that his eyes weren't teasing. Embarrassed, I said, "Thank you."

I thought he would leave right away, but he stayed and told us stories about the theater in Warsaw until the clock struck the seventh hour. Now he is gone, and the clock sits in the center of our table. Its incessant ticking is so annoying that I have covered it with my *pierzyna*, the feather tick that Mamusia made for my bed. The rooster need not worry about losing his job, even if he does make mistakes.

O, Swieta Anno! Most happy mother of the Blessed Virgin Mary, I don't mean to hurry you, but would you please send me a sign soon?

TUESDAY, MAY 26, 1896

Be careful what you pray for. A terrible chain of events happened today, and my fingers are still shaking as I write this. It started when Babcia sent me to buy salt and matches.

As I passed the mayor's office, the squinty-eyed sergeant called to me, "You. Come here." Something in his voice made my legs want to run, but my head knew better. "I found a Gypsy camp today, situated outside the village," he said. "It's interesting the news one learns from Gypsies. Do you want to know what I learned?"

Not waiting for an answer, he touched my hair and said, "I learned that a certain red-haired girl thinks she is above the Czar's law." He paused, studying my face. "I hear this girl teaches school. Polish school. Russian is not good enough for her. You know what the Czar's law says about that."

The sergeant grinned in a mean way, then grabbed my arm and spun me around in one swift, painful movement. He crooked his arm around my neck, saying, "I know ways to get around the law."

His hot breath felt disgusting on my neck. I struggled against him, but his grip grew tighter, choking me. He pulled me into the lane behind the mayor's office. I cried to Saint Ann to help me.

Miracle of miracles, Saint Ann answered this prayer.

She sent Private Nasevich. I don't know where he came from, but he grabbed a stone and struck the sergeant on the head. The sergeant's knees buckled. He fell, a lifeless heap.

"Run, Anetka!" shouted Private Nasevich.

I didn't stop running until I reached my cottage and fell, sobbing, into Babcia's arms. My legs felt as wobbly as the Jablonskis' newborn calf.

"Anetka, what is it?" said Babcia. "What happened?"

I buried my head in her lap. Crying, I told her what the Gypsy had done, what the sergeant did, what Private Nasevich did to the sergeant.

Babcia's hand trembled as she smoothed my hair. "Soldier trouble," she said, her voice shaky.

Within minutes, footsteps crunched outside. Private Nasevich entered without knocking. He came directly over to me, put his arms around me, and held me. "Are you all right?" he asked.

I nodded. At that moment, I felt safer than I had ever felt before.

"Is he dead?" asked Babcia.

"I don't know," said Private Nasevich.

"It would be best if he were dead," said Babcia.

Babcia didn't have to explain. I have never wished anyone dead, but I know that if the sergeant lives, it isn't safe here. Who knows what the Russians will do to Private

Nasevich? Who knows what they will do to me? We would stand little chance in a Russian court.

So our satchels are packed, holding only what we can carry. I have Mamusia's teapot, her ribbons, her apron, my new blouse and chemise, and undergarments. I have Tata's letters, tied with a yellow ribbon. I have my clock. We have filled a basket with three loaves of rye bread and a hunk of cheese. Babcia is sewing our records of baptism and other important papers into the hem of my skirt as we wait for darkness to fall.

Droga Swieta Anno! If you wanted me to go to America, to marry a man I do not know and do not love, did you have to send me stealing out of my village like a criminal?

MONDAY, JUNE 1, 1896
ABOARD THE TRAIN FROM WARSAW

Four days have passed since we left Sadowka. It is the hardest travel I have ever known, and I feel as sore and achy on the inside as I do on the outside.

After our satchels were packed and our papers sewn into my skirt hem, Babcia gave me her crucifix and rosary beads. She also gave me her wooden bead necklace, the one Dziadek gave her on their wedding day. At that moment, I knew she wasn't coming with us. "Babcia," I cried. "I have already lost Mamusia. How can I leave you?"

"This is my village, my home, where my husband, my daughter, and my two baby sons are buried," she said. "What would an old woman like me do in America?"

"What about the soldiers?" I asked.

"Soldiers won't bother an old woman," she said. Then she said to Leon, "Take good care of Anetka and Jozef." She pressed her steamship ticket into his hand.

Babcia offered the few coins she had saved, but Leon said no, that he had rubles enough to pay those people who, for a price, would help us get to the port in Hamburg, Germany. Jozef and I tried to be brave, but we cried anyway. I didn't even get to say good-bye to Stefania.

LATER

Jozef has fallen asleep against Leon, who is watching me with a great deal of interest. He probably thinks I am writing about him. Or maybe he's hoping I will cry so that he will have an excuse to hold me again.

Well, even if I am grateful to Leon for saving me from that sergeant, I am still angry at him for speaking sharply to me today when I called him Private Nasevich. He told me to call him Leon, unless I want to inform everyone that he is a soldier.

No, I won't give Leon the satisfaction of seeing me cry, so I will just sum up the past few days. It was not easy getting to Warsaw. We walked the first night. Then the next day Leon bribed a passing farmer to carry us in his hay wagon, and if you ask me, we paid too much to cross a river in a rowboat. We slept the second night in a haycock.

In Warsaw, Leon found a seedy shop where he paid a good many rubles for passports and other papers. When he saw the worried look on my face, he grinned and said, "The important thing to remember about bribery is never to use it in the wrong place."

See how impossible he is? I am scared and he makes jokes. At the train depot, I held my breath as Russian officers examined every parcel and every passport. (I hid this diary inside my chemise.) I waited to see how many rubles Leon slipped the officers, but he didn't bribe them, not one! Once the officers were satisfied with our passports and belongings, they allowed us to board the train.

I can hardly believe that I have entrusted myself and my little brother to Leon Nasevich, an expert at knowing the right places to use bribery. One minute I think what a low-down scoundrel he is, but then I remember that Saint Ann sent him to save me from the sergeant, and I feel terribly mixed up.

FRIDAY, JUNE 5, 1896
HAMBURG, GERMANY

Since Monday we have been housed in the steamship company barracks while we await our ship. So many people! Austrians, Hungarians, Russians, Lithuanians, Slovaks, Czechs, and Jews, all waiting to immigrate to America.

Most are wearing all the clothes they own. The Hungarian men are easy to identify by their rough jackets and top boots. The Russian men wear belted shirts with tight-fitting collars and bloused trousers tucked into their boots. It is nearly summer, but they wear Cossack hats of fur or lambskin. Most of the men have beards or mustaches.

No matter what country they are from, all the women wear kerchiefs, a wool shawl, and colorful aprons. Some wear boots; others have only felt slippers. One Hungarian woman is wearing ten skirts, all at the same time! She has more bundles and trunks than anyone. She even has a carved rosewood chair. Leon says it is a Hungarian custom for a woman to show off her importance by wearing as many skirts as she can afford. Ten Skirts must be very important in her village.

The voices all sound alike, even if I don't understand the words. I hear crying children, scolding mothers, shouting fathers. I feel so homesick for my grandmother and our cottage that I can hardly bear it. It feels like losing Mamusia all over again.

MONDAY, JUNE 8, 1896
ABOARD THE SS *LIBERTY*

What a sight our ship is! On her uppermost deck, four great chimneys spout black clouds of smoke. Sailors scurry about. Officers stride up and down, barking orders. When we boarded, they watched our bundles carefully, and anyone carrying too much was told to step out of line. Ten Skirts was forced to part with her carved rosewood chair and one trunk. She argued and gestured and pleaded and showed the ship's officer how many skirts she wore, but it didn't matter.

After a health inspection, we were herded like sheep up the wooden gangway, onto a lower deck, then down the stairs. Just when I thought we couldn't possibly go any farther below, I turned and saw another door and more stairs to climb down. Here in the ship's bowels, I can hear the grind of the machinery. I try not to think about how far below the water we are.

For the next few weeks, the steerage passengers will sleep and eat packed in this large room with its low wooden ceiling and wooden floors. A framework of iron pipes forms a double tier of berths. The aisles are so narrow that two cannot pass abreast, and a fight nearly broke out when two men (one wide and one tall) argued over who should give way to the other.

We have each been given a tin pan, a cup, a spoon, and a fork, but no knife. For pillows, we will make do with our hard cork life preservers. I have covered mine with my coat. We each have one thin blanket. With so many people crowded together, I doubt we will be cold.

TUESDAY, JUNE 9, 1896

Lidia and Jerzy Lewandowski have been assigned berths near us. They are Russian Poles, too, from the village of Rawa, near the Bug River. And like us, they are headed for Lattimer, Pennsylvania.

Lidia is eighteen, the same age as Leon, I found out. Her brown eyes and tawny hair remind me of a doe. Doe eyes. Although Lidia didn't say so, I can tell that she is in the family way. If Babcia were here, she could tell whether Lidia's having a boy or a girl. I can't read boy or girl, but I can read the way Jerzy looks at her. His eyes follow her everywhere. Eye love.

Mrs. Mazur is also berthed near us. She has three little children, two girls and a boy, the youngest girl a baby. When the inspection officer asked the children's ages, I heard her say that the oldest boy is ten, though he barely looks Jozef's age. Later she told me that I should have added a few years to Jozef's age. At ten, she said, a boy can work in America.

"I don't want Jozef to work," I told her. "I want him to go to school." That's what Mamusia would have wanted, too.

WEDNESDAY, JUNE 10, 1896

This morning on deck, an important-looking man named Mr. Bogdan offered to teach us English phrases and sentences. He said he is a labor agent for the Pennsylvania Coal Company in Lattimer. He helps Polish immigrants like us find work and housing. He has been back and forth to America five times!

"When I left home," Mr. Bogdan told us, "I was poor, with only a mustache under my nose and a bundle on my back. Now look at me."

Yes, look at him. He is clean-shaven and wears a blue serge suit and a yellow necktie and button shoes with black rubber soles. A derby hat sits atop his shiny bald head. His suitcase is made of the finest imitation leather.

He chews sunflower seeds as he tells us about the officials at Ellis Island who will interrogate us. He has seen immigrants who were rejected and deported to their homelands. To help us, he pretends to be an immigration officer. He asks us questions over and over. "What is your name?" "Can you spell it?" "Who paid your fare?" "Does a job await you?" "Have you been promised work?" "Do you have money?" "How much?" "Are you going to join a relative or a friend?"

He drills us in the right answers to prevent delays and difficulties. When we answer, he asks more questions, harder questions about our political views, our criminal records, and our religion. He tries to get us mixed up, and we argue over the best answers.

"We should tell the truth," says Leon. (This from a person who has bribed nearly everyone from Sadowka to Hamburg!)

"It is better to remain silent and pretend we don't understand," says Mrs. Mazur.

"Then they will think we are stupid," says Leon. "America doesn't want stupid immigrants."

"It is better that they think you are stupid," says Mrs. Mazur, "than to open your mouth and let them know for sure."

And so it goes, back and forth, until the argument comes back to the beginning.

Thursday, June 11, 1896

I have nothing good to write. Each morning we are given hot water to drink, which does no good since only Ten Skirts has brought tea and she won't share. At noon we swallow a bowl of soup dished from a huge kettle. "Mud puddles," Leon calls it. At night we chew hard bread with jam, and at last, we are given real tea to drink. Everyone is hungry, and we talk about the food we will eat in America.

As for me, all I can think about is the husband who awaits me in America. Saint Ann must think he is a good match for me, considering how she sent me from Sadowka in such a hurry! I am trying to get used to the idea, but I have not forgotten that I am angry at Tata. I don't know what I will say when I see him.

Friday, June 12, 1896

Lidia and I spend as much time on deck as we can, for the smell below has grown foul. The steerage reeks of paint, oil, dampness, vomit, and unwashed bodies. It's hard to stay clean with no privacy and with only salt water to wash.

The smell is bad enough for me, but even worse for Lidia, who suffers from baby sickness. At night, I save her my tea so that she can drink it in the morning. It helps to settle her stomach.

Lidia and I are becoming friends. She isn't talkative like Stefania, but I like her serious and quiet ways. Today I told her about Jerzy's eye love. She blushed, but I could tell she was pleased. Without thinking, I found myself saying, "Oh, I hope my husband will love me the way Jerzy loves you."

I hadn't meant to say the words out loud and was shocked when I heard myself. I was even more shocked at what Lidia said. "I have seen the way Leon looks at you," she said, touching my arm. "He loves you already."

"I'm not marrying Leon," I blurted out. "I'm marrying Stanley Gawrych. My father has arranged a marriage for me in Lattimer."

Lidia turned bright red from embarrassment. "Oh," she said in a small voice. "I'm sorry for my mistake."

Leon has eye love for me? Isn't that the most ridiculous idea!

SUNDAY, JUNE 14, 1896

Since we have no priest, we held our own religious service on deck today. We recited the rosary, touching each bead to keep count as we repeated the Our Father, Hail Mary, and Glory Be. Leon did not say the prayers, but when we finished, he told a story about Jonah, who tried to run from his duty to God. Jonah fled on board a ship, but God found him and sent a huge storm to punish him. To calm the sea, the sailors threw Jonah overboard, and he was swallowed by a whale. After three days and nights, Jonah repented. God spoke to the whale, and it spit Jonah out onto dry land.

I think I know how Jonah felt. Jozef loved the story, though I don't think it fitting for people at sea to hear.

MONDAY, JUNE 15, 1896

Lidia told me a secret today. She wanted to marry Jerzy, but her parents refused to allow it for they had arranged a marriage to another man. Desperate, she and Jerzy found a priest in another village who agreed to marry them. When her parents found out, they tore open the ticking of her feather mattress and threw the feathers to the wind. She cried as she told me that, and I understand why, for it means her own mother and father have disowned her.

THURSDAY, JUNE 18, 1896

Jozef has a habit of disappearing for hours. When he returns, he always has something to share — cheese, or an orange, or an apple, or a sandwich. Today he had a rich lady's tapestry handbag. I knew the handbag belonged to someone and had to be returned, but my curiosity overcame me. I had never seen such a handbag. What could it hurt to look?

Jozef shook the contents onto my bed. Such fancy things fell out: a silver comb and hairbrush with soft bristles, a round silver case, a jar of chalky red powder, a tiny glass bottle filled with amber water, a white jar, and a white pocket handkerchief trimmed with pink lace and embroidered with the letters *LRF*.

I picked up the silver case and pressed a small button. The lid snapped open to reveal a mirror on each side. My hair was a mass of tangled coils, and my face was sunburned and freckled. I looked ugly enough to scare a wolf.

Leon happened by as I opened the jar of chalky red powder, and I found out he knows all about ladies' things. He told me that some ladies use the powder to give their cheeks color. Next I opened the glass bottle and sniffed it. What a powerful smell! Leon said that some ladies wear the perfume on the back of their wrists and behind their ears. I asked Leon how he knows what ladies wear, but he just grinned. When he wasn't looking, I dabbed perfume on my wrists and behind my ears.

Last, I unscrewed the lid to the white jar. The milky-white cream smelled like roses. I rubbed some on the back of my hand. The texture felt soft and smooth, but not nearly the quality of the bag balm Babcia makes for our milk cow.

I imagined out loud about the sort of lady who owned this handbag. "She probably owns clothes enough to change every day of the month," I said. "She probably goes to fancy parties and dances."

"You should see her," said Jozef. "She wears a frilly pink hat and long gloves the same color as her hat. She always has a fellow on each arm."

Leon looked at my brother sternly. "How do you know that?"

Jozef clamped his mouth shut and looked away.

"Answer Leon," I said. "How do you know about the lady who owns this handbag?"

Jozef looked me in the eye, and I saw the horrible truth: My brother had stolen this handbag and he wasn't the least bit sorry.

Leon spoke to Jozef in a voice I had never heard before, a voice that reminded me he was a soldier. "It must be returned immediately," he said sternly, taking Jozef by the collar. "Come. We will find a ship's officer."

Jozef didn't argue. Now they are gone, and I have

scrubbed the perfume from my wrists and from behind my ears. I am scared. What if someone finds out about Jozef? He will never be allowed into America.

FRIDAY, JUNE 19, 1896

I do not like Mrs. Mazur. She reminds me of a crow, with her baggy black dress and sharp eyes. When she sees me writing, she rolls her eyes in a mean way. Today, while we were on deck, she said that book learning makes a girl unsuited for marriage.

She makes me angry. I told her that I am suited for marriage, that someone does want me for a wife, that a good match awaits me in America. "No doubt my husband is a rich and kind man," I said. "Rich and kind enough to ask no dowry and to pay for our passage." That shut her beak. I felt glad, but Leon got a cross look on his face. He went over to a group of men who were smoking pipes and playing cards.

I left Mrs. Mazur and stood by the ship's rail. I thought about that old crow and what I had said to her. Suddenly, I didn't feel so glad anymore. Sure, I had answered her smartly, but what if she is right? What if I am unsuited for marriage? What if my husband does not approve of me? What if he cannot love me?

I looked at the ocean. All I could see was gray — gray sky, gray seas. I tried to imagine where Sadowka lay, somewhere behind me. At that moment, I missed Babcia so much that I longed to swim home.

Soon Leon came and stood by me. He smelled of pipe smoke. "Mrs. Mazur is wrong," he said. "In my opinion, book learning makes a girl all the more suitable for marriage." His eyes were soft, not teasing at all. He moved closer, and our arms touched, and I remembered how safe I felt in his arms the night he rescued me from the sergeant.

For a second, I let my guard down and said, "If I were to jump overboard, I think I could swim home."

His eyes grew softer, then quickly turned teasing again. "If anyone could swim back to Sadowka," he said, "it's someone as headstrong as you." He tilted back his head and laughed.

Droga Swieta Anno! Do you see how he tries my patience, Dear Saint Ann? I entertained a pleasant thought of pushing him overboard to see how far he could swim. Maybe a whale would swallow him.

SUNDAY, JUNE 21, 1896

Mass this morning. I prayed and prayed to Saint Ann that Stanley Gawrych and I will be a good match.

MONDAY, JUNE 22, 1896

Jozef disappeared again today, but this time he found a mother cat and her three kittens, hidden in a dark corner underneath the stairs on an upper deck. We made them a comfortable bed beneath the stairs in our compartment and fed bread and cheese to the mother. Leon says the ship has cats to keep mice and rats away from the food.

The kittens' eyes are open, and they walk on shaky legs, the way I walked the first few days at sea. The smallest one has long black hair and white boots. I nuzzled her face, and for a minute the hollowness I had been feeling in the past few days went away.

Jozef picked up a gray striped kitten and turned it over. He looked at the kitten's squirming bottom and said, "I still can't read the stamp. What does it say?"

WEDNESDAY, JUNE 24, 1896

Droga Swieta Anno! I am ruined. I cannot face anyone, and just lie in my berth. Lidia asks me again and again what's wrong. I tell her that I have stomach sickness, when in truth I am sick from shame.

After dinner last night, a man announced it was Saint John's Eve, marked by the summer solstice, when the sun gives the earth its longest day and shortest night. "Dance! Dance!" he shouted.

Several men brought out violins, trumpets, wooden horns, tambourines, and even a small accordion. At first, only the men danced, raising their arms and shouting and stamping and clapping. Soon women and girls joined in.

It made me homesick as I remembered how our village celebrated Saint John's Eve. We built a bonfire on the hilltop and danced and sang until the flames died low. Then each marriageable young man picked his favorite girl. Holding hands, they leaped across the embers. If they landed still holding hands, everyone knew they would soon marry.

We had no bonfire on the ship, but the men and women, boys and girls danced as if their feet were on fire. Suddenly, Leon hooked his arm around my waist and pulled me into the circle. I could scarcely catch my breath. When the dance was over, Leon didn't let go, but pulled me away from the circle and kissed me on the mouth.

That kiss traveled down to my feet. I felt as though they were stuck to the floor. When they became unstuck, I pulled away and ran back to my berth, where I threw myself onto my mattress and burst into tears. Saint Ann, I feel so ashamed. How could I have done such a thing? How can I face Stanley Gawrych?

Friday, June 26, 1896

For two days, Leon and I have stepped around each other, careful not to bump, saying, "Excuse me" and "Pardon me" and "Would you please" in the most cautious voices.

This morning, Leon found me holding the black kitten. He crouched next to me and said, "I'm sorry."

I glared at him. "One dance did not give you the right to kiss me."

"You're right," he said. "It did not."

"At last," I said, "we can agree on something."

And then he had the nerve to say, "I think we agreed on something else."

"What?"

He grinned. "That kiss."

O, on jest trudny! He is impossible! It was a shameful kiss. How dare he think for one minute that I liked it!

Saturday, June 27, 1896

Last night I dreamed Leon kissed me again. I felt his arms around me and his breath on my neck, and I curled into those arms and felt loved. Then suddenly I woke up and realized it wasn't a dream. Someone's arms *were* around me. Someone *was* breathing on my neck. Someone *was* in my bed.

I gasped and bolted upright, hitting my head on the berth, which knocked some sense into me. The someone was Jozef. He had crawled into my bed. "I had a bad dream," he murmured.

At times like those I forget how troublesome my brother can be. I tucked his blanket around him and kissed his forehead and hummed the lullaby Mamusia used to sing when I had bad dreams.

When he fell back to sleep, I rolled my blanket, pressed it against him for comfort, and slipped out of bed. I wrapped my coat tightly around me and went over to the kittens. The black one crawled out to me. I took her upstairs to the deck. Here in the gray morning light, I am sitting, huddled with the kitten beneath my coat, the cold wind snapping around me as I write.

Saint Ann, what kind of girl am I, knowing that I am to marry Stanley Gawrych but liking the feeling of that dream and those arms?

SUNDAY, JUNE 28, 1896

After Mass today, the boat engines suddenly stopped. "What is it?" "Is something the matter?" "Is something wrong with the boat?" All kinds of stories started up, but then someone shouted, "America!"

I grabbed Jozef's hand. We hurried up the stairs and crowded onto the deck. Far off, I saw a jagged line. Land! It was America. I hugged Jozef and started to cry. I spotted Leon, and he grinned and nodded.

Soon the Statue of Liberty came into view. We pushed against the rail to get a glimpse. Mothers and fathers lifted their babies and small children so they could see. There were cheers and laughter and more crying. People crossed themselves and prayed.

Leon pushed his way over to us and lifted Jozef to his shoulders. The Statue of Liberty looked sad and lonesome. She reminded me of a saint, and I don't know why, but I was suddenly filled with sadness, too. I could not take my eyes off her mournful face. What kind of place is this America, I wondered as our ship floated past a harbor. Tall buildings loomed in front of us.

Then the moment was gone, and it was rush, rush, rush. Ship officers strode up and down the decks, barking orders and directions. "Hurry up! Quickly! Run! Over here! Over there! Men here! Women there! Children with the mothers!" Identification tags were pinned onto our clothing, and we were herded onto a smaller boat and transported to a great inspection hall.

At the hall, a stern and sour inspector checked our papers. Ten Skirts became flustered when she had to remove eight skirts to cut the papers out of their hems.

Nobody in America cares how many skirts you can wear. They only care if your papers are in order.

In another hall, we were poked and prodded and interrogated. Our eyelids were pulled up, our chests and backs thumped, our legs and fingers, hair and scalp examined. They even measured the beating of our hearts.

Then the dreaded chalk mark! When a doctor found something suspicious — redness of the eyes, or lameness, or a cough — he marked a letter on the foreigner's coat. Oh, the wail that went up each time a coat was chalked.

To our great relief, there was no chalk mark for Jozef, Leon, or me. Now we are sitting, waiting to answer more questions to see if we will make suitable Americans.

LATER

I cannot believe it has happened, but America does not want Leon Nasevich. I was standing behind him as an inspector questioned him about his political views. With each response, the inspector's frown grew deeper. It went something like this:

Inspector: "Are you a Socialist?"

Leon: "I believe in individual freedom."

Inspector (frowning): "You are an anarchist, then?"

Leon: "I believe all should contribute to the good of the community."

Inspector: "Are you guilty of any crimes?"

Leon: "Yes."

Inspector: "What crimes?"

Leon: "I was a soldier for the Czar, and because of that, I am guilty of crimes against humanity."

The inspector made furious scribbles in his notebook, then said, "Come with me."

Leon shoved a bundled-up shirt at me and said, "I'll be all right." The inspector grabbed Leon's arm and led him away.

I stood dumbfounded, holding Leon's shirt. My throat tightened, and I thought I was going to cry. At that moment, something squirmed inside the shirt. It was the black-and-white kitten, trembling and mewing.

Oh, Leon, why didn't you keep your mouth shut and let the inspectors think you are stupid?

I am writing this as I sit on a train headed for Lattimer. After the last inspection, Mr. Bogdan tagged us with more identification papers and the addresses of our destinations, as if we were big parcels, and took us to the train depot. The train windows are painted black — so no one will be tempted to get off before Hazleton, says Mr. Bogdan with a snorting laugh. He laughs, but I think it's true!

I wish Jozef would stop bouncing on the seat. I can hardly write! He says he is looking for Leon, even though I have explained again and again that Leon has been deported. Jozef insists that I am wrong, that Leon will find us.

The kitty is asleep on my lap, curled on Leon's shirt. She has eaten bits of a meat sandwich I saved from my breakfast at Ellis Island (the only meal we were given!). Now her belly feels round and full. I have decided to call her Buty, because her paws look like little white boots.

Saint Ann, why do I miss Leon so? Every time I look at Buty and think of Leon, my chest feels tight and I want to cry. I shouldn't feel this way. He is troublesome to have around, and he torments me. Even America doesn't think he is suitable.

STILL LATER

The conductor says we are nearly in Hazleton, the city closest to Lattimer. Lidia is asleep, her head on Jerzy's shoulder, I am glad she and Jerzy are going to Lattimer. It will feel good to have a friend, someone who can help me with husband questions.

I am trying not to stare at Lidia and Jerzy, but sometimes I think if I can just copy everything she does, say everything she does, that I will know how to be a wife whom a husband can love. Lidia does everything so gently. She talks in whispers. She listens carefully. It's hard to remember to do those things. Babcia always said I rush out to greet the world instead of waiting for it come to me — just like Mamusia.

I remember what Babcia said, that love is not important in a marriage, that the match is more important than love. But I look at Lidia and Jerzy, and think, Why shouldn't a marriage be a good match *and* loving? If labor pains awaken mother love, what awakens marriage love?

Oh, I feel nervous. So nervous! What will I say when I see Tata? Part of me wants to run into his arms, the way I did when I was a little girl. The other part wants to yell that he had no right to trade me for tickets.

MONDAY, JUNE 29, 1896

We are a family again. It is late, but I will try to write it all down, starting with how we arrived at the Hazleton train depot. A group of American boys greeted us. They threw sticks and stones and hollered, "Hunky! Hunky!" at us.

Mr. Bogdan shook his fist at them and hollered English words back. Jozef stooped to pick up a rock, but I yanked his collar. The boys ran away. "*Glupi* Americans," said Mr. Bogdan. "They call you 'hunky,' and you're not even from Hungary!"

Another company agent joined Mr. Bogdan. They told us to climb into a hooded wagon, and we did, fast! I was glad the wagon was covered so the American boys couldn't see us. I could not stop shaking. All the short ride to Lattimer, I held Buty close and thought about the American boys and the ugly faces they made. What did we do to deserve that?

When we arrived in Lattimer, we were taken to the company boardinghouse where Tata stays. I like Mrs. Szarek, the widow who runs the boardinghouse. She is a mushroom of a woman, with a wide body and skinny legs. She says Tata is a good man, full of kindness. I felt proud.

We moved our belongings into the house. The downstairs is one large room. At one end, a large pot was simmering on a stove. It smelled like onions and cabbage. In the living area, I counted five beds and eight trunks. Over each bed, a crucifix and pictures of the Virgin Mary and patron saints are hung. Two men slept in one bed with their clothes on. Mrs. Szarek explained that they work the night shift at the coal mine, which means they sleep during the day. Another man sat in the corner, sounding out words in an English spelling book. Narrow steps led to an upstairs.

"I have no bed for you," she told Jozef and me. "Everyone here shares. You will share the floor."

Mrs. Szarek brought us tea and black bread with huckleberry jam, a piece of cheese, and a saucer of milk for Buty. Suddenly a scream pierced the air. *O moj Boze!* I prayed to God and crossed myself.

"That's the breaker whistle," Mrs. Szarek explained. "It tells the mine workers when to start and when to quit each day. The first time I heard that whistle, I hid under my *pierzyna*."

She led us outside and pointed to a tall, gloomy, black structure that rose in the valley to the north of the boardinghouse. The breaker looked like a monster, its head rearing against the sky. Even from where we stood, I could hear the rumble of its machinery. A group of black-faced boys emerged from the breaker.

Soon mine workers covered in soot straggled past the boardinghouse in groups of two and three. Their eyes looked like full moons against their blackened faces. "Let's see who spots Tata first," I told Jozef.

My heart felt like a thundercloud as mine workers straggled by. I could not wait to see Tata, but at the same time, I remembered how angry I was at him. What would I say? What would he think when he saw that Babcia was not here? What would he say when I told him about Leon?

Suddenly, I caught my breath as I saw a man with the same square build and medium height as Tata. He walked with a plodding gait that seemed clumsy like a bear, but that I knew could dance the most graceful mazurka.

He stopped in the street. His eyes searched my face, then Jozef's, then mine again. He blinked, rubbed his eyes. *"Moje dzieci!"* he shouted, his voice unsteady. "My children! Anetka, Jozef, is that really you?"

Jozef and I leaped off the porch and ran to him.

"*Dobra! Dobra!*" said Tata. "Fine! Fine!" Tata cried as he squeezed us, pressing us against him.

At first, it felt as though I were hugging a stranger. He smelled of dampness and oil and dirt and something that reminded me of rotten eggs. But beneath that smell was Tata's own smell — tobacco, whiskey, garlic sausage, and hard work. I cried as I hugged him back.

Later I cried again as I told him about Babcia. "*Biedna Babcia,*" he said. "Poor Babcia. Your grandmother is a stubborn old woman." But I could tell he missed her.

TUESDAY, JUNE 30, 1896

Something is wrong. Tata cannot look me in the eye when I ask about Stanley Gawrych. After dinner, Tata said, "Come outside — time for a talk, you and me."

We walked in silence down the crooked dirt path to the coal patch shanties where the married mine workers live with their families. The ramshackle houses look as though a good wind might scatter the boards. They all need some nails and a good whitewashing. I felt homesick for Sadowka, its thatched roofs, its whitewashed cottages, its hedge fences.

A year of missing words hung between Tata and me, and I felt each day as we walked. It took Tata forever to get around to my marriage. First he pointed out the different sections of the patch village, where the Italians live, the Hungarians, and the Poles. The immigrants are clustered together near others from their homelands, where they can speak their own languages and practice their own customs. The noisy alleys seemed alive with children. Boys were playing ball in the lanes. Girls were carrying buckets of water and minding babies and small children.

Next Tata pointed out the gardens. Every available space behind each shanty is planted with cabbages, beans, corn, potatoes, turnips, and more. The best gardens grow behind the Italian shanties. "See that?" said Tata pointing to a round red fruit. "It's a tomato. We never had tomatoes in Sadowka. And see the sunflowers? Just like home."

Lattimer is nothing like home, I wanted to say, but instead I said, "Mamusia always cut a sunflower to decorate the crucifix and holy pictures of the Blessed Mother." I wondered if Tata remembered.

He smoothed my hair with his broad hand. "You are the vision of your Mamusia." He looked away, studying the sunflowers. "We were a good match, your Mamusia and I. That's what's important in marriage."

I wanted to ask Tata if he loved Mamusia, if marriage love ever came for them, but the words wouldn't come. I swallowed hard and said, "When will I meet Stanley Gawrych?"

"Saturday, the Fourth of July," said Tata, not looking at me. "It is a big American holiday. No work, just picnics, races, horseshoes, and baseball."

We walked back to the boardinghouse in silence. Why can't Tata look me in the eye? What is he not telling me?

WEDNESDAY, JULY 1, 1896

Tata's letters never told us how dangerous coal mining is! As I helped Mrs. Szarek bake bread this morning, she told me about a terrible disaster that happened just three days ago at the Twin Shaft mine in Pittston, a town not far from Lattimer. A massive amount of rock and coal fell. Fifty-eight men are feared dead. Over one hundred children are fatherless. "What will the mothers do?" I asked Mrs. Szarek.

She clucked her tongue. "Some will go back to the old country. Some will send their children to work. Some will find new husbands. When my husband died, I took in more boarders."

THURSDAY, JULY 2, 1896

Mrs. Szarek sent Jozef and me to pick coal at the culm banks. The culm banks are large black mountains of loose

rock from the breaker. Most of the rock is slate, but some coal can be found, too. The banks surround Lattimer, the coal mine, and its buildings.

Jozef and I pushed the creaking wheelbarrow along the dirt road. We met up with other women and their daughters. Some were Poles like us, but most were Hungarians and Italians.

Mrs. Szarek warned us not to climb near the top, where the culm is loose. She told us about a woman who suffocated when the culm gave way beneath her feet and buried her. I had to look constantly after Jozef, who always seems to be where he shouldn't be. We filled the wheelbarrow with coal, and now Jozef is sitting outside, cracking each chunk into small pieces for the coal stove.

FRIDAY, JULY 3, 1896

Tomorrow I meet Stanley Gawrych. My stomach feels so nervous! I tried to ask Mrs. Szarek about him, but all she said was, "Don't worry! You are young like I was when I married my husband, but you will make a fine wife and mother. I always know these things."

I visited Lidia. She and Jerzy are boarding with the Wozniak family until they can afford to rent their own company house. Lidia tried to calm me down and assure me that any man is lucky to get me for a bride. She made me some tea to settle my stomach, but it hasn't helped and just keeps me running to the outhouse.

SATURDAY, JULY 4, 1896

I have celebrated my first American holiday, I have seen my first baseball game, and I have met Stanley Gawrych. Now I know why Tata couldn't look me in the eye.

This morning I made extra-thick sandwiches of hard-boiled eggs and cheese and sausage. Mrs. Szarek gave me a jar of pickled cucumbers and a chunk of sweet cake. We carried the picnic lunch out to a field and sat on a bank, watching the older boys and men play a game called baseball.

I tried to watch the game, but I couldn't bring myself to care how far a grown man can hit a ball or how fast he can run when I was waiting to meet my husband-to-be. Before long, Tata and Stanley were there, standing in front of me, and I was being introduced. My heart pounded hard enough to beat a hole through my chest.

I tried to read Stanley the way Babcia would. Stanley is tall. He is strong looking with light brown hair and thick eyebrows. He has an agreeable face though he doesn't smile much. His teeth are white and straight. I am glad, for I would not want to kiss a husband with crooked yellow teeth. He doesn't smell bad, and his neck is clean. His hands are clean, but his knuckles and fingernails are lined with black coal dust, just like Tata's. Stanley's eyes are dark brown and don't tease, and I hope that means he won't be impossible like Leon — a good sign, I am sure.

I spread out the picnic blanket and passed out the sandwiches. Stanley chewed slowly as he watched the baseball game. I worried that maybe he was eating slowly because he didn't like his sandwich, but he ate it all, every crumb. I was about to ask him if he wanted another sandwich, but he said, "Anetka, do you like children?"

The question surprised me, and I noticed that Tata swallowed hard. "Yes," I told Stanley. I wanted to tell him about the children I taught, but I didn't get the chance. He cut me off, saying, "Come with me."

Tata nodded permission, still not looking at me. Stanley led me across the field, past Mrs. Szarek's, and down the path to a wooden shanty that seemed tidier than the rest. He opened the front door, and I stepped into a kitchen that held a large table, two chairs, two long benches, and a stove. The room was neat and orderly, the floor swept. A doorway led to a small room. Narrow stairs led to a loft.

Footsteps pattered upstairs, then three faces appeared over the side of the loft. "There's someone I want you to meet," Stanley told them.

Three little girls hurried downstairs. They stood by Stanley and looked at me with serious faces and solemn brown eyes. "Anetka," said Stanley, "meet my daughters — Violet, Rose, and Lily."

Daughters! The word roared in my head. Not knowing what else to say, I said, "What a beautiful garden." The smallest one, Lily, buried her head in her father's trousers. The middle girl, Rose, giggled, but the oldest one, Violet, gave me a hateful stare.

LATER

Nobody asked me if I wanted to come to America. Nobody asked me if I wanted to be a wife. Nobody asked me if I wanted to be a mother. And tonight, without even asking me, Tata and Stanley and Father Dembinski settled on a wedding date. My wedding will take place three weeks from now, Saturday, July 25.

"A good match," said Father Dembinski.

"A good match," said Tata, looking proud.

Stanley nodded. "A very good match."

I looked at all the smiling faces — from Father Dembinski to Tata to Stanley — and I prayed to Saint Ann that they are right.

Mrs. Szarek brought out a loaf of rye bread and two white scarves. Stanley took my right hand and held it.

Tata bound our hands together with the scarves. Stanley's broad hand felt rough and strong as it closed over mine.

"Stanley and Anetka are now joined together," said Tata, "and through their joining will always have bread beneath their hands."

Our engagement is now as binding as any marriage contract. Stefania and I often talked about what it would feel like to be engaged, and I waited to be filled with some kind of feeling. But other than the roughness of Stanley's hand, I felt nothing. Just numb.

Stanley and I sliced the bread. I gave slices to Rose and Lily and took one over to Violet. She was sitting on the steps, holding Buty in her lap. "Do you like kittens?" I asked.

"No," she said, pushing her from her lap. The kitten rubbed against Violet's legs. I could tell Violet longed to hold Buty, but she wouldn't give in to me. What a stubborn six year old!

"I like kittens," said Rose, who is four.

"Me, too," added three-year-old Lily.

Soon the shanty porch was crowded with the boarders. Others came as the good news spread — the Wozniaks, the Mazurs, the Poteras, Jerzy and Lidia, and other faces I didn't know. They all toasted us and gave us their blessings. As I took in the blessings and toasts, I could hear Babcia telling me that being a wife and mother was a girl's highest calling, her sacred duty.

I looked over at the girls. Rose and Lily were eating their bread, but Violet was gone. With dismay, I saw her bread squashed on the ground.

SUNDAY, JULY 5, 1896

We all walked to Mass in a bunch — Stanley, his girls, Tata, Jozef, and me. Jozef refused to walk with *girls* and ran ahead.

Here is something I noticed. When the miners come home from work, they all look alike, their faces black with coal dust. But today, dressed in their best clothes for Mass, they all look different. The Italian men wear dark trousers, short jackets, and round little hats of black felt. The Slovak and Polish men wear stovepipe pants, white shirts, and slouch hats. The women wear head kerchiefs and long baggy dresses. I saw an Italian wife who looks younger than me!

Each foreigner goes to his own church. The Italians go to the Church of Precious Blood, the Slovaks go to Saint Joseph's, and the Poles go to Saint Stanislaus's. "Only in America will you see so many people going to so many different churches," said Tata.

All during Mass, Jozef sat far away from Violet, Rose, and Lily. He got a sour look on his face as Father Dembinski proclaimed Stanley's and my first banns of

marriage. The banns must be announced three times before our wedding, to allow for anyone who objects to our
marriage to come forward.

During the sermon, Father Dembinski said that God
has a plan for each of our lives. Lily looked at me shyly,
then climbed into my lap and sat there the whole Mass.
Rose leaned her head against me. Violet ignored me. I
thought about Sophie, Stanley's first wife, who died after
giving birth to a stillborn son. I prayed to Saint Ann to
help me see God's plan and to fill me up with sacred duty
and high calling. These little girls need a mother.

After Mass, I told Stanley that I want to watch his girls
while he works. I could tell he liked that.

MONDAY, JULY 6, 1896

Violet was not happy to see me this morning, especially
when I moved some of my belongings into the shanty. I put
my teapot and clock on a shelf next to the kitchen stove.
She fussed that she wanted to go to Mrs. Wozniak's, the
way the girls always did when their father worked. But
then she saw Buty. "Your father said the cat can move in,"
I told her. Violet's eyes brightened, and she decided to stay
after all but tried not to look happy about it.

Since today is wash day, I decided to wash their clothes.
I have never seen such dirty pants as Stanley's coveralls!

They were caked with coal dust and mud. I spread them on the washboard, rubbed them with soap, then scrubbed them front and back with a brush. The water turned black.

The same black coal dust coats everything — the fence, the grass, the trees, the garden. In the distance, the coal breaker rumbles, sending up more black clouds. A coal train waits outside the breaker. Car after car is heaped with hard, black coal. Lattimer is a bleak patch village, with its noisy breaker, black shanties, and dangerous culm banks. It's nothing at all like Sadowka.

I reached into the washtub, up to my elbows in water, and wondered if Babcia and Stefania were also doing wash at that very minute. Suddenly, I was filled with that homesick feeling and wanted nothing more than to be home in Sadowka. I missed my grandmother. I missed Stefania, too, and the meadows where we picked flowers, the woods where we climbed trees, and the river where we fished in the summer and skated in the winter.

Before I knew it, I was crying. Lily hugged my leg, and Rose asked what was wrong. I just hugged them back and rocked them the way Mamusia used to rock me until I felt better.

Tuesday, July 7, 1896

Mrs. Szarek, the girls, and I carried pails up the mountain and picked huckleberries. It felt good to leave the blackness of the patch village and walk among green bushes and tall grass.

As I watched the girls pick berries, I tried to picture what their mother must have looked like. The three girls have brown hair and brown eyes like Stanley, but Violet has long, heavy lashes, dark to the very tips. She squints and furrows her brow as she works. Then she looks just like Stanley. Rose looks like Violet, but she smiles a lot. She is a hard worker. I could tell by the way her little fingers expertly pulled the berries. Lily has curly brown hair. She ate more berries than she picked.

In my head, I put together a picture of Sophie. Perhaps she had curly hair like Lily, deep brown eyes like Violet and smiled a lot like Rose. As I was thinking that, I noticed that Violet was humming a lullaby about an old gray goose, a lullaby that Mamusia used to sing to me. I started to hum along, but Violet glared at me. "You don't sing it right," she said.

By early afternoon, we had filled four tall pails. We sold the berries for five cents a quart to the huckleberry peddler, who waited with his wagon outside the company store. I gave a penny to Violet, Rose, and Lily to buy candy.

As the girls picked out their candy, Mrs. Szarek said

to the clerk in English, "Fifty pound flour, ten pound sugar, put on book." I recognized the words *fifty pound flour* and *ten pound sugar*, but not *put on book*. The clerk opened a big leather book and scratched something in ink. I could not get over how Mrs. Szarek did not pay the clerk. She just told him to "put on book."

Outside, a beer wagon rattled down the street. Mrs. Szarek hefted the flour onto her shoulder. "Hurry," she said to us. "It's quitting time."

I don't like quitting time because I don't like helping the boarders with their baths. They strip out of their mine clothes, then kneel beside the washtubs. Mrs. Szarek and I scrub their backs with worn-out underwear, but they wash the rest themselves. Mrs. Szarek bosses them to wash the backs of their hands and behind their ears. No matter how hard they scrub, they can't wash away all the coal dust.

WEDNESDAY, JULY 8, 1896

This morning Jozef complained about breakfast and wouldn't wash his face. At the culm bank he climbed high on top and pretended not to hear my *girl's* voice when I hollered at him to get down. He wouldn't fetch water because *girls* were at the well.

When he refused to crack coal because it was *girls'* work, I wanted to crack him. I scolded him and told him he was setting a bad example for the girls. He called me a bossy old hen and said he hated me. Then he hollered, "Why don't you just get married today?" He took off, nearly bowling Lidia over as she came up the path.

I hurried over to ask if she was all right, then apologized for my brother and told her how difficult he has been. Lidia listened quietly then said," Maybe it's his way of saying he doesn't want to lose his sister."

"O jej!" I said. "How can he think he's losing me?"

She didn't say any more. She squeezed my hand in a way that said, Think about it, Anetka.

Lidia left, and I did think about her words. I plopped down next to the coal. I must face the truth. Soon I won't be Anetka Kaminska anymore. I will be Mrs. Gawrych, wife and mother. I feel as though somebody else is walking around inside my skin. If Jozef thinks he's scared of losing me, how does he think I feel about losing myself?

The more I thought about how lost I felt, the angrier I became. I picked up Jozef's hammer and cracked a piece of coal. I cracked another and another, and pretty soon I was crying and cracking coal and it felt good.

LATER

When Jozef came home, he was in better spirits. I was glad to see that but not glad to hear why. He puffed himself up like a rooster and told Tata and me that the breaker boss said he is big enough and fit enough to pick slate. Jozef starts tomorrow.

To make matters worse, Tata looked pleased that Jozef had gotten himself a job. "Jozef needs to go to school," I told Tata. "He needs to learn English and to read and write."

"He can learn English while he works," said Tata. And that was that.

Later, Mrs. Szarek tried to comfort me. "Jozef may think you're bossy," she whispered, "but he will find out soon enough what it means to have a real boss."

I find no comfort in that. I know what Mamusia would have wanted. She would have wanted Jozef to go to school.

THURSDAY, JULY 9, 1896

This morning Jozef washed his face, allowed me to smooth his hair into place, and ate breakfast, all without complaint. He laced his hobnail boots, grabbed the lunch pail I handed him, and hurried to catch up with several other boys headed toward the coal breaker.

All day I fretted and worried about Jozef so much that I had no time to worry about my wedding. At last the breaker whistle blew, and I watched for him.

When he saw me, he hid his hands behind his back and ducked his head. Something was wrong. "Show me your hands," I said. He looked at me. His face was black with soot except for two white trails down his cheeks. My brother was crying.

I grabbed his hands and gasped. His fingers were swollen, cracked, and bleeding. He blinked back his tears, tilted his chin, and said defiantly, "We aren't allowed to wear gloves. The boss said once my fingers toughen up, they won't bleed anymore."

Uparty brat! Stubborn brother! I led him inside and poured his bathwater. When he was done, I slathered goose grease on his fingers and wrapped them in soft cloths. Soon Tata and the other boarders were home. They teased Jozef about his red tips, and I could tell he liked the attention.

Mrs.Szarek said red tips are caused by the sharp edges of the coal and slate, which cut the skin. The sulphur blasting powder also causes the skin to swell and crack open. It will take two weeks for his fingers to toughen up.

FRIDAY, JULY 10, 1896

Two weeks until my wedding! I prayed extra hard to Saint Ann to fill me up with high calling and sacred duty because I don't seem to be filling up on my own. The closer my wedding date gets, the more the idea of being a wife and mother scares me down to my toes.

If Saint Ann thinks that sewing underpants is a high calling and sacred duty, then my prayers were answered. Mrs. Szarek gave me three leftover flour sacks made of soft white cotton with tiny blue flowers and told me to cut out new underpants for the girls and myself. So I did, even though I hate to sew. When I showed the underpants to Mrs. Szarek, she remarked that I did a good job. I wished out loud for pretty lace to trim the leg openings.

"We'll buy lace in Hazleton," said Mrs. Szarek. She whispered to me, "We're only supposed to trade at the company store, but they charge too much. So we'll go to Hazleton. Bosses don't scare me."

Lidia offered to watch the girls, and Mrs. Szarek and I walked into Hazleton. I am not used to cities like Hazleton, with its wide, tree-lined sidewalks, carriages, and shops, and men hurrying in all directions. We went into a dry goods store where I picked out soft blue lace at three cents a yard.

A pretty American woman worked behind the counter. She is Lidia's age, I think, and wore a pale green dress with rows of tiny white buttons and puffy sleeves. Her dark hair was swept into a knot on top of her head. She pressed a loose strand into place, and I noticed her hands were red and chafed.

Our eyes met and suddenly I felt clumsy and ugly in my old baggy skirt, worn blouse, and head kerchief. I paid for the lace and hurried from the store. All the way home, I thought about her hands.

LATER

It is late. The light is dim and my eyes are sore, but the underpants are all sewn up and trimmed with lace. I wrote a letter to Babcia and described the underpants to her. I know my practical grandmother will raise her eyebrows at the blue lace, and it makes me laugh to imagine the village priest reading this letter to her.

I still need a wedding present for Stanley. I don't think he will want fancy underpants!

SATURDAY, JULY 11, 1896

Mamusia used to tell me that sometimes we need to give up the life we have planned to find the life God has planned for us. Today I planned to pick huckleberries, but then I heard the low drone of wings.

"Look!" I said to the girls. Before our eyes, hundreds of bees descended upon a hollow old tree. The bees carried large pellets of yellow pollen on their hind legs. The tree was humming with bees.

I left the girls at the boardinghouse and returned to the hollow tree with a knife, an axe, matches, a pail, and a piece of rotten wood. I lit the wood and urged the smoke into the hive. Once the bees were drowsy from the smoke, I cut open the trunk with an axe, exposing a glorious hive, large and filled with capped cells of honey. With the knife, I cut away the top and sides, robbing as much honeycomb as I could without destroying the hive. I hurried home with a full pail. I crushed the honeycomb and hung it in cheesecloth to drain.

As I watched the amber honey dripping into the pail, my heart felt good to know bees again. To celebrate, I took the girls to the company store and let them pick out five cents' worth of candy. Their eyes widened in delight, and I felt pure pleasure.

To the clerk, I said in English, "Put on book."

He looked at the girls. "Gawrych?" he said.

I nodded, surprised that he knew their name, but I guess the coal companies know everything about the people who live in their homes and work at their mines. The clerk opened his leather book and wrote something down. As I watched the girls eating their candy, I felt sacred duty and high calling.

SUNDAY, JULY 12, 1896

Second banns of marriage announced today.

I showed Stanley the pail of honey. He asked questions about the hives I kept in Sadowka, and I told him about the mornings and afternoons spent hunting bees and tending hives with Mamusia. He was impressed, I could tell, and I caught him looking at me sideways. I thought he was going to kiss me, but he didn't.

I suppose it is a good sign that he didn't kiss me, for it shows he respects me (unlike *somebody else*, who thought that one dance gave him the right to kiss me!). But now I have been thinking about kisses all day, and I wonder if Stanley's kiss will stick my feet to the floor.

MONDAY, JULY 13, 1896

Stanley's poor cow! Her milk bag is cracked and swollen. I buttered my hands but could not persuade her to let down her milk. She needed Babcia's bag balm. As I melted the beeswax and fat on the stove, I found myself remembering the jar of good-smelling cream from the boat, and that, in turn, made me think about Leon. I wonder where he is, and I hope and pray that he is all right, even if he is too much of a scoundrel to be an American. It also gave me the idea to make a nice-smelling balm. Babcia's recipe doesn't call for mint oil, but I couldn't see what it could hurt. I snipped some mint from Mrs. Szarek's garden and put the leaves in a small jar with some oil. Tomorrow I will add nicely scented oil to the balm.

TUESDAY, JULY 14, 1896

I made another batch of balm today. This time I strained the melted beeswax and fat extra fine, then added the mint oil. The bag balm smells like a tiny leaf, and the texture feels better than the cream in the lady's tapestry handbag. Satisfied, I spooned balm into a small jar, then cut a square from a flour sack. I fit the cloth over the top and tied it in place with a piece of leftover lace.

I scrubbed my face and neck and hands, then dressed in a clean blouse. Mrs. Szarek frowned when I told her I was going to Hazleton. She didn't like the idea of me walking by myself, but she saw my mind was made up, so she offered to watch the girls.

In Hazleton, I found my way to the dry goods store. Up close, the American woman looked even prettier. For a second, the clumsy and ugly feelings swelled inside me again, and my feet wanted to run but I didn't. Her red, chafed hands needed my balm.

I rubbed some cream onto the back of my hand, then motioned for her to try some. She hesitantly stuck her pinky into the balm and rubbed it onto her hand. She sniffed her hand and looked pleased. "How much?" she said in English.

Through nods and hand motions, I explained as best I could that the cream was a gift. If she liked it, I would bring more for her to buy. It took some patience, but at last we understood each other. It felt good.

SATURDAY, JULY 18, 1896

Glupia! Glupia! I feel foolish and stupid. Today was pay-day, and Stanley came home furious. "The company store has cheated me," he said. "They deducted fifteen cents for candy. We've never had candy."

"We have," said Violet.

Stanley looked at me, shocked. "You bought candy?"

"Put on book," I said, in English.

"Put on book!" he hollered in Polish. He went on and on about the company store, how "on the book" means the coal company deducts the cost from his wages — the same as they deduct for anything else he buys, such as blasting powder, squibs, oils, and other mining supplies.

I began to cry, and he calmed down a bit. "Didn't you know this?"

"No," I said. "How could I know?"

Violet looked pleased that I was in trouble.

Sunday, July 19, 1896

Last night I dreamed that Leon was sitting in the back of the church. When Father Dembinski proclaimed our third banns of marriage, Leon objected. He popped to his feet and told everyone that he had kissed me.

I awoke, feeling a shameful mixture of fear and longing for Leon. I reminded myself that it was a ridiculous dream. For one thing, Leon has been deported. Besides, even if he were in America, he is the sort of man to sit outside church and read a book. Later, as I walked to Mass with the others, I felt glad that Stanley is the sort of man to sit in church — a very good sign for a husband, I am sure.

Monday, July 20, 1896

I made another batch of mint balm and took five jars to Miss Ada Mackinder, the pretty American woman. She looked so happy to see me that I thought she might leap over the counter. She pushed up her dress sleeves and showed me her hands. Nearly all the redness was gone.

This time we settled on a price for the balm. I left the store with three yards of fine white cotton, enough to make Stanley a wedding shirt, and had nearly seventy-five cents left over. On my way down the street, I counted the jars of cream and pounds of honey I could sell if I had wooden bee boxes, the sort I had in Sadowka. My head full of bees, I tripped right into a man. "Why, Anetka," said the man in very crisp, very polite Polish. "We have a habit of bumping into each other."

I looked up into Leon Nasevich's grinning face, and that is *all* I am going to say.

TUESDAY, JULY 21, 1896

I will say this: Leon is an impossible man, a low-down scoundrel whom America should have had the sense to keep out. But he was never deported, only detained. Now he has gone ahead and invited himself to my wedding. He says he wants to thank Stanley personally for the steamship ticket. He says he brought the bride over, and that entitles him to a dance. He walked away before I could uninvite him!

WEDNESDAY, JULY 22, 1896

I have not seen Stanley these past two evenings. He has been busy since Monday, working on a wedding surprise for me. He will not even let me down to the shanty but sends the girls up to the boardinghouse to stay with me during the day.

Before dinner tonight, the girls asked to visit the mules at the colliery, so we walked to the mule stable and watched as the drivers brushed down the sturdy-looking animals. I feel sorry for the mules, who had been underground since early morning, dragging the heavy coal cars up the slope, even though Tata tells me the mules are treated better than the men.

THURSDAY, JULY 23, 1896

Only two days until my wedding, and I am growing a terrible case of nervous bride jitters. I have never missed Mamusia more.

I tried to ask Lidia if there is anything I need to know about marriage, but she had her hands full at the Poteras', helping with the five little ones, since Mrs. Potera was doing poorly from the birth of her sixth baby girl. Every time I tried to ask Lidia about marriage, she'd say, Hand me this, or Hand me that, or Can you believe that Mr. Potera is angry with his wife for having another girl? He hasn't even asked about the baby, but sits outside drinking himself drunk and calling himself an unlucky man.

I helped Lidia, then found Mrs. Szarek. She was kneeling in the garden with a can of kerosene and water. She turned over a potato leaf and shook two potato bugs into the kerosene. When I asked her if there is anything I need to know, she squinted up at me and fired off a list of questions. "Can you butcher a hog? A chicken? Can you cook? Can you clean? Tend babies? Plant a garden? Put up jars of berries and vegetables for winter? Smoke sausage? Put up a barrel of sauerkraut?"

"Yes," I told her. "But is there anything else I need to know?"

Mrs. Szarek thought a moment. "No, that's about it," she said.

I busied myself with Stanley's wedding shirt. The sides and sleeves are stitched, and now I have the buttonholes left to sew. *O jej!* I hate buttonholes.

FRIDAY, JULY 24, 1896

Tomorrow is my wedding day. Stanley showed me my wedding present: three wooden bee boxes. "They didn't cost anything to make," he told me proudly. "I found the scrap lumber and nails around the colliery. And did you know that honey sells for ten cents a pound?"

I didn't know that, and never in my life did I expect such a fine present. I examined each one, lifting the lids, checking the entrances. The hives were just as I had described, and it sent a thrill through me to think that Saint

Ann has sent me such a thoughtful husband. It made me want to kiss him, but I didn't because the girls were there. I must set a good example for them.

I gave Stanley his shirt, and he remarked how well it fit and how well it was sewn. Rose and Lily loved their fancy underpants. Before I could stop her, Lily stepped out of her old ones and changed right there in the yard! Violet complained that the lace itched and refuses to wear them. Thank goodness I have had lots of practice with an ornery brother, or I would never manage Violet.

SUNDAY, JULY 26, 1896

Yesterday was our wedding day. Jozef and Tata dressed in their best trousers and shirts and Sunday shoes. Jozef's face was red from Mrs. Szarek's scrubbing. Tata's mustache was neatly trimmed and freshly waxed. Mrs. Szarek wore a simple dress with tiny embroidered flowers.

Lidia fussed with my hair. She untied my braids and combed them out, the way Mamusia used to do. It filled me with an achy feeling, and I burst out crying and said I wished Mamusia were here. Lidia hugged me and stroked my head, saying, "You have your mother in your heart. You will carry her with you always."

Lidia pulled my hair into a tight bun and helped me

finish dressing. I wore the blouse that Mamusia had sewn for me and a full black skirt. I also wore the wooden beads Babcia had given me, the ones she wore on her wedding day. Then Lidia left me alone to finish my prayers to Saint Ann and the Virgin Mary. I prayed hard for them to bless my marriage.

During the wedding Mass, my knees trembled, and when Father Dembinski pronounced us man and wife, it sounded like the ocean roaring in my ears. Rose and Lily said, "Are we married now?" And I told them, "Yes, we're married." They put their little arms around my neck and squeezed. Violet, of course, wouldn't.

After the Mass, Stanley and I rode in a decorated wagon back to Mrs. Szarek's. Everyone brought food and drink. So much food! Pierogi and smoked sausage and spareribs and fish! Golabki and kolduny and beef tongue! Crullers and chrusciki the way Babcia made them! Soups and breads and a honey wedding cake that took forty eggs and two men to carry it on a board! Fat barrels of beer and whiskey lined the porch.

Tata's friends played their violins, trumpets, accordions, and drums for us. Oberek, polka, mazurka — we danced them all until sweat ran down our backs and faces. I danced with Tata, then Rose and Lily. Violet and Jozef sat by themselves, looking gloomy, refusing to dance no matter how many times I asked. Loud enough for them to hear, Mrs. Szarek said it will be a wonder if those two don't end up married. Jozef and Violet steered clear of each other the rest of the night.

Soon it grew time for the wedding dance. Mrs. Szarek sat on a chair, and the men lined up and dropped coins in her apron for the privilege of dancing with me. I was caught and whirled until my head spun.

Just when I thought there was no one left to dance with, Leon appeared. He pulled me into the dance circle, his arm around my waist, and we whirled about the room. When the dance ended, there, in front of everyone, he kissed me on the hand. It may as well have been on my lips, the way that kiss traveled up my arm and down to my feet. My feet felt stuck to the floor, just as they did on the ship.

Stanley pushed through the crowd. His jaw was tight, and his face grew red. Leon looked him straight in the eye, never flinching, and I felt electricity spark between them. Then Stanley grabbed my hand and pulled me away. Holding my hand high, he led me back to the center of the guests. Leon went over to the whiskey barrel, dipped himself a glass, gulped it down, and left without looking back. I don't know why I felt hollow inside, but I did.

Soon it was time to leave. The men and women teased us as Stanley carried me from the boardinghouse. Outside, he set me down and held my hand as we walked in the darkness to our shanty. The girls were staying with Mrs. Szarek for the night.

Outside the shanty, Stanley kissed me. It was a plain and simple kiss, nothing at all like Leon's. I wanted to ask Stanley to kiss me again, because I hoped a second one might stick my feet to the floor, but I didn't.

Stanley carried me over the threshold to our tiny bedroom near the kitchen. Some things are too private to write even in a diary of private thoughts, so all I will say is that I became a married woman, and it wasn't at all like I expected. Afterward, I wondered if I should kiss Stanley goodnight, but he turned his back to me and went to sleep. I laid awake for the longest time, missing my mother.

TUESDAY, AUGUST 18, 1896

Stanley and I have been married nearly a month, and I can see it has been some time since I have written in my diary. Taking care of a house and husband and three little girls leaves me worn out.

At night I collapse into bed, so tired from all the washing, scrubbing, cooking, sewing, picking coal, wiping noses, and wiping bottoms (Lily still needs my help in the outhouse) that I can't bear to think that when I wake up, I have to do it all over again. Every minute of my day is spent taking care of somebody else.

I was hoping that by now, Tata and Jozef could move their things down from Mrs. Szarek's, but Stanley told

Tata that if he and Jozef expect to board here, they can expect to contribute their wages, same as any other family member.

Tata grew red in the face and shouted, *"Psia krew! Dog's blood! I will pay only one dollar a month to board at my own daughter's house, the same that I pay to Mrs. Szarek."*

"It is my house," said Stanley. "Not Anetka's." It made me mad to hear that.

WEDNESDAY, AUGUST 19, 1896

Violet fusses and complains until I feel like pulling out my hair. Whatever I tell her to do, she does the opposite. She teases her sisters until Rose flies into a rage or Lily cries and hangs onto my skirt. Some days, I can't even go to the outhouse without Rose or Lily banging on the door, screaming for me to hurry up because Violet is tormenting them. At times like these, I miss Mamusia. She would know whether to hug that girl, ignore her, or turn her over a knee and spank her.

Thursday, August 20, 1896

Last night a terrible roof fall occurred in a Coleraine mine. Nobody was hurt, but Violet looked distressed. "Are the mules all right?" she asked.

Stanley snapped at her, saying, "Bosses care more about mules than men. It costs money to replace a mule. Men they get for free."

I don't know why Stanley had to use that tone. "Yes," I told her, "the mules are all right."

"Oh," she said. "I'm glad."

No sooner did she find out the mules were safe than she pinched Rose. The pinch led to a slap, the slap led to hair pulling, and before I knew it, the two girls were rolling on the floor, punching and kicking. Since Violet started it, I put her in a corner and gave her a pile of potatoes to peel for supper. It is puzzling to me how that girl can care so much about a mule but torment her own sister.

Saturday, August 22, 1896

A large black snake was found near the schoolhouse. An Italian man clubbed it and carried it on a pole through the streets of Lattimer before it died. The snake measured five and a half feet long.

Now Violet thinks that a snake is reason enough not to start school on Monday. I told her she must learn to read and write English. "You're not my mother," she said in a hateful voice. It will be a relief to have Violet in school all day.

MONDAY, AUGUST 24, 1896

Violet always waits until her father is gone before she starts to fuss and act ornery. Today she wouldn't get dressed, then she said she wasn't going to school because I wouldn't let her wear shoes. I told her firmly that she needs to save her shoe leather for the cold weather. When she realized I wasn't giving in, she got herself dressed but wouldn't let me help with her hair.

The next thing I knew, she had somehow managed to get the comb tangled in her hair. She wailed that she could not go to school with a comb stuck in her hair, and all I could think of was, Did she do it on purpose?

Finally, I tried oil to ease the comb from the tangles. To my relief, it worked. Violet calmed down, and as I brushed and braided her hair, I hummed the lullaby about the old gray goose that Mamusia used to sing to me. Suddenly, tears rolled down Violet's cheeks. "What's wrong?" I asked her.

She didn't want to say, and I thought she was fussing

about the snake again, but then she said in a tiny voice, "Mama used to sing that song. When I close my eyes, I remember Mama brushing my hair."

I hugged Violet. She stiffened at first and tried to pull away, but when I wouldn't let go, she melted right down. I told her how I cried on my wedding day when Lidia brushed my hair, because it reminded me of my mother. "Do you still miss her?" she asked.

"Co dzien," I told her. "Every day."

She let me wipe her nose and wash her face. I held her hand as we walked to the schoolhouse. By the time we got there, she didn't want to hold my hand anymore, and she was back to her ornery old self, complaining about the snake and no shoes. I felt glad.

WEDNESDAY, AUGUST 26, 1896

The last time I made bread, Stanley said the crust was too dark and didn't I know how to bake. Today as the bread baked, I covered the tops with brown paper, the kind the butcher wraps the meat in, and the loaves turned out light-colored. I felt clever.

I clipped the weeds and grass around my three bee boxes that sit on stands near the fence by the garden. The fence is tall enough so that the line of bee flight is well above the heads of horses and drivers. Beneath one box, a hen has made her nest and it has three eggs. I like to hear the thrum of the bees as they work, and I imagine that it sounds like a lullaby to the mother hen and her chicks.

SUNDAY, AUGUST 30, 1896

Most Saturday nights we gather on Mrs. Szarek's porch. Last night, Tata and Stanley grunted a few words at each other, but that's all. My husband and father are stubborn men! The Mazurs, Wozniaks, and Lidia and Jerzy were there, too.

Lidia and Jerzy sat close to each other, nuzzling and holding hands, the way two people shouldn't do in public, even if they are married. Seeing that made me feel lonesome, since Stanley won't nuzzle me even at home. If it weren't for Rose and Lily, I'd have nobody to hug at all.

The men chipped in for a barrel of beer. Sometimes they tell stories about the ghosts they hear while at work in the mines. The ghosts are mine workers who were killed. Last night, the men talked about their wages, their bosses, and the company store.

Mr. Mazur was angry because the company store charged him for coveralls he never bought. When he complained, the clerk told him, "You better keep quiet if you want to keep your job."

Mr. Wozniak told how his Irish boss assigned him and several other Polish men to "monkey holes." The boss, he says, doesn't like Poles or Italians and calls them all sorts of names. When a boss doesn't like a worker, he assigns him to a bad spot where the coal is difficult to reach or a vein isn't thick, and they have to work extra hard to earn the same amount of money. In a monkey hole, the workers crawl on their hands and knees through narrow tunnels to reach the coal. They must drag along their tools and the wooden props to hold the roof.

Stanley's mine foreman is a tough Welshman who drives Stanley and the other foreigners crazy, keeping them blasting and shoveling right up until the breaker whistle blows.

As I watched Stanley, I tried to imagine what it's like for him, working like a worm underground, feeling the weight of a mountain overhead. Stanley is one of the luckier men, since he is a miner, the man responsible for setting the powder and blasting the coal. He learned when he worked as a butty to an American miner. Now the laws have changed, and very few foreigners can become miners. The most they can hope to be is a butty, the miner's helper.

"You men deserve more money," said Mrs. Szarek. "Especially when you are forced to work where the coal is harder to mine."

"More money, ha!" said Stanley. "We should live to see the day."

"My husband was assigned to a bad spot once," said Mrs. Szarek. "The water in his chamber was knee-deep. I told him to tell the foreman that he deserved extra pay."

"What happened?" asked Stanley.

"The foreman refused, saying the water wasn't as deep as he claimed," said Mrs. Szarek.

"See?" said Mr. Mazur. "Bosses don't listen."

Mrs. Szarek chuckled. "So my husband picked up the foreman, carried him to his chamber, and threw him into the water. He didn't get extra pay, but at least the foreman knew how deep the water was."

Everyone laughed, and the men started to talk about what they would like to do to their bosses, especially the new mine superintendent, Gomer Jones. The men call Gomer Jones the worst slave driver ever to set foot in the coal region, worse than all the Irish and Welsh foremen put together.

Mrs. Szarek said, "You need to stick together against bosses like Gomer Jones. You need to teach bosses like him how to treat you."

When I look at Mrs. Szarek, I am sure she could teach the bosses a good lesson or two.

Stanley still won't kiss me afterward in bed at night. He turns over and falls asleep, and soon I'm lying there, listening to him snore.

As I carried a full milk pail from the cow shed this morning, I was caught by the sunrise. It stretched along the purple mountains like a yellow and orange ribbon. The morning felt cool, but the grass was shiny wet with dew, and the air smelled moist and green. It reminded me of a morning in Sadowka, and I wondered if Babcia was also holding a full milk pail at that moment. It always comforts me to think that our hands are doing the same work, even though we are an ocean apart.

When I went inside, Stanley sat at the table drinking his coffee. *"Co za piekny poranek,"* I told him. "A beautiful morning." I tried to hug him, but he slid past me the way he always does, as if last night never happened. You would think that when two people have been close in the night, they would carry the feelings with them the next day.

"Might as well stay dark," he grumbled. Then he pointed to this diary lying on the table. He picked it up, opened it, and said, "What's this scratching about?"

I felt insulted. My handwriting does not resemble scratching. Mamusia took great care to show me how to slant and loop the letters. Then I remembered that Stanley does not read Polish, not one word, so I explained that I write my private thoughts in my diary.

"You have thoughts important enough to write down?" he said with a laugh. For the first time, I noticed that his laugh comes from the top of his throat, not his belly, like Leon's. Stanley snapped on his coveralls and plunked his miner's hat on his head.

Outside, he joined Mr. Wozniak and Mr. Mazur. The men didn't say a word to one another. They just watched their feet as they trudged toward the colliery.

I doubt if they saw the sunrise, or smelled the air, or heard the birds. I think I understand why, when I imagine how they will spend the next ten or twelve hours in darkness, blasting the coal, shoveling chunk after chunk into mine cars, wondering if they will live to hear the breaker whistle.

I wonder where Leon is working.

SATURDAY, SEPTEMBER 19, 1896

An American huckster tried to sell me some bad fish today. I don't know much English, but I know bad fish when I smell it. "No good," I told him. "No good for dogs."

He sneered at me, said a few words, and climbed aboard his wagon. I guess nobody else wanted to buy his fish either, because the next thing I knew, he was hollering and throwing the entire wagonload of fish all through the alleys and lanes. The smell is sickening. I wish I knew more English to tell that huckster what I think of him.

MONDAY, SEPTEMBER 21, 1896

This morning I wrote a letter to Stefania. I described my wedding to her and told her the truth about married life, that married life is nothing like I had dreamed. Then I ripped up the letter and burned it in the stove.

WEDNESDAY, SEPTEMBER 23, 1896

The mornings are growing cooler, and soon the first frost will come. I collected the last of the honeycomb, about twenty pounds from each hive. When Violet came home from school and saw the honeycomb, she worried that the bees would go hungry. I assured her that I had left enough for the bees to survive the winter. That satisfied her. Then she asked me if I would teach her to hunt bees next summer. Of course I will, I told her. I would like nothing better. After that, she was nice to me and her sisters for a good hour but turned back into her ornery self by dinnertime. Saint Ann, are we making progress?

Thursday, September 24, 1896

I sold half the honey — almost thirty pounds — but kept the rest for us to enjoy over the winter. I also made ten jars of scented balm from the wax. While Violet was at school, I asked Lidia to watch Lily and Rose. I walked to Hazleton and sold all the jars to Miss Mackinder.

When Stanley heard that later, he scolded me, going on for the longest time about how dangerous it is to walk by myself, and don't I know not to be foolish. He kept on about the terrible things some Americans do to foreigners and how I need to be careful.

I did not like being scolded as if I were a child. "Yes," I told him, "I know how to be careful. I was always careful in Sadowka, where I walked everywhere by myself." In my mind, I saw that horrible sergeant's face. I pushed the thought down and changed the subject to Miss Mackinder and how she had bought my scented balm.

A funny look crossed Stanley's face. "How much did she pay?" he asked. I don't know why, but something told me to show him only half the money. When I dropped the coins onto the table, Stanley didn't complain about my carelessness anymore.

The beer wagon rattled outside. Stanley grinned and pocketed the money. It made me angry, seeing him leave like that and knowing he would drink the money away. I

felt glad that I had kept half the coins. I will send them to
Babcia to help pay her taxes.

TUESDAY, SEPTEMBER 29, 1896

The rattle of the Black Maria is the darkest sound in the
world. I was canning mushrooms when the black-covered
death wagon clattered down our street. It made me tremble. The death wagon always takes me back to the morning Mamusia died.

I ran to the doorway. I crossed myself and whispered
an Our Father, and Rose gripped my skirt as the wagon
stopped in front of the Wozniak shanty. I cannot describe
the relief I felt that it did not stop in front of ours.

"They took Mama away in a wagon like that," said
Rose in a tiny voice. Her little body shook. I knelt and
hugged her tight.

Mrs. Wozniak screamed and sank to her knees as the
driver and another man carried her husband's burned
body on a long wicker basket into the house. He and
three other miners died when the flame on his lamp
touched a dangerous gas called firedamp. The gas exploded, sending out flames and searing heat. I remembered how, just this morning, Mr. Wozniak and Stanley
had walked to work together, their eyes watching the

ground and not the grass or trees or sky. Now Mr. Wozniak is dead.

I lifted my heavy pot off the stove, and as the mushrooms cooled, I took two loaves of bread and a jar of peaches over to the Wozniaks. Mrs. Wozniak is very angry at her husband for dying and at the company bosses for letting him.

WEDNESDAY, SEPTEMBER 30, 1896

Last night the sky darkened and the wind picked up, turning leaves over on the trees. I latched all the window shutters, and as it poured rain with lightning and thunder outside, Rose and Lily snuggled close. Violet didn't snuggle but sat at my feet, and I hummed and told stories to comfort them. Storms always make me feel sad and wistful, but this one felt sadder than usual as I thought about *biedna* Mrs. Wozniak, who has to sit up with her husband's body. This morning, I saw much storm damage throughout Lattimer. In the Italian section, a shanty was blown down and boards scattered everywhere. Another family lost their chimney.

FRIDAY, OCTOBER 2, 1896

A beautiful funeral Mass was said for Mr. Wozniak today. All his fellow miners turned out, even though it meant losing a day's pay. His tools have been raffled off, which gives his widow a bit of money. I am glad Lidia and Jerzy still board with Mrs. Wozniak.

THURSDAY, OCTOBER 8, 1896

At night, Rose and Lily help me strip and pull feathers. I am making a feather *pierzyna*, big enough to cover Stanley and me. I don't have enough feathers saved yet, but I can add to them each year. As we work, Violet does her schoolwork. She already knows her letters and sounds out simple English words. By watching and listening, I am slowly learning, too. Most foreign women in Lattimer know only enough English to get by at the company store. I want to know more, so I can haggle better over prices and make sure I am not cheated.

WEDNESDAY, OCTOBER 14, 1896

This afternoon Lidia paid me a visit. She looks so happy and content. She put my hand on her stomach and let me feel the baby kick. When I felt it, my throat tightened and it made me wish I could talk to Lidia about married life. Married life is nothing like I had hoped. It is much harder than I ever imagined to take care of a house and husband and three little girls, and I am left with precious little time for myself if I wish to conduct myself in a manner that won't make Stanley cross.

The other men brag about Stanley's talent for mining, how he can sense a weak roof or the dangerous gas. I don't know why Stanley can't sense my feelings. He does more hollering than talking. Last night he hollered because I didn't have a growler of beer waiting for him. (I missed the beer wagon because Lily had an accident and needed my help in the outhouse.) Then he didn't like the soup and said the butcher cheated me and didn't I know how to pick out a soup bone. He thinks I am a *leniwa zona*. I am not a lazy wife!

At night I can't even play with the girls without getting a scolding look from him if we giggle too loudly. When I fall into bed, I wish Stanley would hug me or hold my hand, but he won't.

FRIDAY, OCTOBER 23, 1896

Yesterday I put up 150 heads of cabbage that I bought from a farmer. I bought a barrel from the company store, and Rose helped me roll it home. I scrubbed it, scalded it, and set it in the sun to dry. Then I spread a clean sheet on the kitchen floor. I put a board across two chairs and began to slice the cabbage, first in half, then in thin slices.

By the time Stanley came home, the chopped cabbage lay in a big pile on the sheet. I helped him with his bath and spent extra time cleaning his feet, for it is the husband's job to tamp the cabbage.

I dumped a bushel basket of cabbage into the barrel and salted it, and Stanley climbed in. I said a little prayer, asking the Lord to bless our work, the same prayer Mamusia used to say when she and Tata made sauerkraut.

Stanley walked in a circle, tamping down the cabbage. As he walked, I added more cabbage. When the barrel was half full, he told me to give him a bracer, and I poured him a glass of whiskey. He tamped and braced himself until the barrel was full and the whiskey bottle was empty.

By the time I fit the lid onto the barrel, Stanley was so woozy from all that tamping that he flopped onto the bed. He pulled me onto the bed with him, planted a slobbery kiss on me, and said, "We made good cabbage, Sophie." Then he fell asleep and never woke up, not even for dinner. The girls and I pushed the barrel into the corner of the kitchen and laid three heavy stones on top to keep the lid in place.

After the girls went to bed, I paced for a good long while, thinking how Stanley had called me Sophie, his first wife's name. I feel sad and lonesome to think he had marriage love for Sophie but does not for me.

MONDAY, OCTOBER 26, 1896

The house stinks from the fermenting cabbage. Lily walks around pinching her nose shut. Soon the cabbage will be ready, and we will move the barrel into the cellar.

Now that winter is coming, I can hear mice setting up housekeeping in our walls and floorboards. Last night their little feet made scratching sounds, sure signs they are building their winter nests. This morning I invited Buty inside. Within an hour, she brought me her first mouse. I am glad Violet was in school and did not see the poor dead thing, or she would have cried for sure.

THURSDAY, OCTOBER 29, 1896

Stanley brought some sad news home tonight. Gas exploded in a Wilkes-Barre mine today. The explosion was felt a mile away at the mouth of the shaft. Six men are dead, including three men from the rescue party. Most were married with children.

I feel bad for the dead men, but I feel worse for their widows and children. It makes me think about Mrs. Wozniak and how hard it is for her to make ends meet without her husband's wages. Her oldest boy has quit school to work in the breaker. The oldest girl is nine, and she also has quit school. She found a job housekeeping for a Welsh family in a big white house with a spacious yard on Quality Road.

SATURDAY, NOVEMBER 7, 1896

More sad news. A terrible boiler explosion occurred this morning in a Centralia mine. Five men were badly burned by the scalding water and injured when they were thrown by the blast. Four of the men are expected to die.

TUESDAY, NOVEMBER 10, 1896

I had finished ironing and was just sitting down to write in my diary when Lidia knocked at my door. I invited her in, poured her a cup of tea, and said, "Should you be out with the baby's time so near?" I could see that the baby had dropped and that Lidia was carrying much lower.

She laughed, saying she had so much energy that morning that Mrs. Wozniak had nothing left to wash, fold, or iron. Then we talked about poor Mrs. Wozniak and how she is working herself to death taking laundry in. Nearly every woman at church is playing matchmaker, hoping to find her a husband.

Suddenly, Lidia gasped and clutched her side. The next thing I knew, she was sitting in a puddle of water. "Anetka!" she said in a scared voice. "The baby's coming."

I sent Rose and Lily to stay with Mrs. Szarek then helped Lidia down to her shanty. Mrs. Wozniak and I got Lidia to bed.

I have never helped birth a person, only calves or kittens and once a litter of pigs. I tried to remember everything Babcia ever told me. I unbraided Lidia's hair, for the Blessed Virgin Mary rushes to a woman's side if her hair is unplaited while she is in labor. I unlocked all the chests and doors, because knots and locks increase the pain of childbirth. Then I sat by Lidia so she could pull on my hand when the pains got really bad.

Lidia and Mrs. Wozniak did the rest. Lidia struggled the whole morning and into the afternoon. As the pains grew worse, she squeezed my hand so hard I thought the bones would crack. But finally, she gave a push and moaned, and into Mrs. Wozniak's hands slid a wet, squirming, squalling baby boy. The first thing he did was pee.

Mrs. Wozniak put the baby on Lidia's chest, and it

struck me that Babcia was right. Labor pains do awaken mother love. I could not help myself — I was choked with tears.

I helped Lidia wash up, and Mrs. Wozniak prepared the hazel water for the baby's first bath in the wooden bin that Lidia makes bread in. She taped a silver dollar over the baby's belly button and swaddled him in a blanket.

Lidia was nursing the baby when Jerzy came home. Oh, the eye love! He kissed his son, then bent over Lidia and kissed her forehead and held her. I was choked with tears all over again as I wondered how it would feel to be loved like that.

By the time I got home, Stanley was sitting at the kitchen table. Before I could tell him about Lidia, he started in on me that there was no dinner, and the cow needed milking, and what was I doing all day. Then he spotted my diary, picked it up, and shook it in my face, saying, *"Leniwa zona!* My lazy wife has time to scratch in this but no time to put dinner on the table?"

The beer wagon rattled outside, and he didn't wait to hear about Lidia or to eat dinner. I banged pots and pans and made the girls a hurried meal. While they ate, I took my diary and the milk pail out to the cow shed. The cow mooed when she saw me coming. I knew she was eager to be milked, but I told her she didn't want my fingers pulling at her until I had written my anger out.

Droga Swieta Anno! Please help me. I know Stanley

works hard all day, but I don't understand why he is so short-tempered. I am trying to be a patient and loving wife and mother, but he doesn't appreciate anything I do. From now on, I will find a private place to keep my diary.

Sunday, November 29, 1896

It has grown too cold to sit outside when we meet at Mrs. Szarek's, so we crowd inside. Tonight Mr. Mazur brought up the subject of the United Mine Workers union. He said the union is a good thing, that it can fight against the company stores and help pass laws to protect the mine workers, especially the foreign workers. Tata said that thirty cents dues is too much to pay, and Stanley agreed. Mrs. Szarek said that union or no union, the mine workers have to organize and stand up to their bosses. Then the talk about Gomer Jones began, just like every other Saturday night.

I grew bored hearing the same talk as always, so I slipped away to visit Lidia and the baby. After a mother gives birth, she cannot leave the house or take a real bath for forty days. Once the forty days have passed, Lidia will go to church for a special blessing for mothers, and the baby will be christened.

Lidia looked tired but happy. Since we were alone, I

heated water on the stove and helped her with a sponge bath. She told me that she and Jerzy have picked a name for the baby, but she couldn't tell it to me since it is bad luck to reveal a baby's name before the christening.

Friday, December 4, 1896

Last night it snowed. The snow blows through the cracks of the shanty. I warmed six bricks in the oven and put three in the girls' bed and three in ours to keep us warm. This morning the men were out early, shoveling the path and the lane to the schoolhouse. I heard them talking, a mixture of Italian, Hungarian, Polish, and bits of English as they shoveled the snow together.

Saturday, December 5, 1896

We were visiting Tata and Jozef tonight when Violet reminded Jozef that night school is starting at the schoolhouse. Jozef shot her the dirtiest look and said he will not go. He said he is learning enough English, and when he said a few words, Violet's eyes grew large. Later she whispered to me that they were bad words. Curses. America is changing my brother, and I wonder what will become of him.

He hangs around with tough-looking boys who strut about with their hands in their pockets. Some of the boys are Polish, but others are Italian and Hungarian.

THURSDAY, DECEMBER 10, 1896

I mailed *Oplatek* to Babcia and Stefania and sent them good wishes. I hope the blessed wafer arrives in time for Christmas.

At night the girls and I make blown eggs and straw figures to decorate our Christmas tree. Stanley isn't worried about Christmas presents for the girls. He says they will understand that Saint Nicholas doesn't have enough gifts for all the patch children after he stops at the big houses on Quality Road. I don't want to tell the girls that, so after they go to bed, I stay up late, sewing three little rag dolls.

It is getting harder and harder to stretch Stanley's pay from month to month. Last month he made $38, but he owed $26.28 to the company store, $11 for blasting powder, 38 cents for smithing, and $4.50 for rent. So this month he is still in the hole $4.16. If he didn't drink so much beer, it would be easier for us to manage.

Monday, December 14, 1896

I hung the wash to dry in the loft. Then I gathered my sewing and bundled up Rose and Lily, and we visited with Lidia and the baby. Soon his christening will be here, and then we will know the name Lidia and Jerzy have picked for him.

Motherhood seems so natural to Lidia. I wondered out loud if it will come naturally to me. "You are a good mother already," said Lidia.

"The girls are big enough to tell me what they want," I told her. "But how will I know what a baby wants?"

Lidia smiled. "You will know," she said confidently. "When the baby cries, you nurse him. When he fusses, you burp him. When he wiggles, you change him."

Some people say you spoil a baby by holding him too much, but when I see how contented Lidia's baby is, I don't think that you can ever hold a baby too much.

Tuesday, December 15, 1896

As I was making soap today, I got it in my head to make a good-smelling soap for the girls. I experimented with different oils, honey, beeswax, and other ingredients. Now I have tiny bars of coffee soap, tea soap, honey and oatmeal soap, and even a soap that smells like pine trees. I hid them under my bed to cure.

SUNDAY, DECEMBER 20, 1896

Little Roman Lewandowski was christened today. Jerzy must have spent a month's salary. The Wozniak shanty was filled with a dozen kegs of beer, several gallons of whiskey, boxes of cheap cigars, and food, food, food. A man dragged out the worst sounds from an old accordion, and we all danced, hopping on one foot, then the other in the crowded shanty.

It felt good to celebrate, and everyone had too much to drink. The more we drank, the more we shouted and danced and sang. I became so light-headed that when I spotted hulking shapes in the darkness outside, I didn't pay attention. Suddenly, the shanty door flew open as though a mule had kicked it in. Three American men burst inside. They were as drunk as the Polish men.

The accordion player stopped. I rushed to the girls and pushed open a window. "Hurry," I said. "Outside. Go home." Lidia grabbed little Roman. She climbed outside, too, and I passed the baby to her.

I knew I should leave, but something — perhaps fear — stiffened my legs. The first man had a flat, sour-looking face, but he was thick and powerful. He said something in

English to Stanley, and Stanley said something back that the sour man didn't like. Then Stanley's eyes brightened, and he flew into action so fast I could hardly believe what was happening. With one hand, Stanley tossed his drink into the man's face, then threw a punch with his other hand that caught the man in the jaw.

Five more Americans piled inside. Everywhere I looked, fists were flying, men were falling, men were dodging fists and bottles and chairs. A brown-haired man reached up for Stanley, and he grasped the man's wrists and flung himself backward, dragging the man with him. On his back, Stanley caught the man in the stomach with his feet and threw him over, sending him flying. The man landed against the wall in a flat spraddle.

Stanley jumped to his feet, dodged another man's blows, and managed to stick his fist into another man's mouth. Jerzy kneed another American, who collapsed with a low groan. Mr. Mazur dragged him outside.

"Tata, look out!" I screamed. Too late. The sour-looking American clamped Tata's arms from behind, pinning them behind his back. Tata stomped the man's foot with his heavy workboot. The man winced but held on tighter. Another American, slow but strong looking, pulled back his huge fist to slam Tata in the face. He never made it.

Stanley reached out with one broad hand, grabbed the man by the shoulder, and spun him around. He drove a fist into the American's throat, and the man fell, choking and gasping for air. As Stanley turned to face the American holding Tata, the American let go and headed out the door. The others followed.

The fight was over. Everyone was quiet, then I heard weeping. Mrs. Wozniak was crying. Her table and all her chairs were broken. Glass lay everywhere, and the front door was torn from the hinges. I went over to her and hugged her. "What am I going to do?" she cried. I tried to reassure her that her friends will help.

We cleaned up as best we could, and Stanley set the door on its hinges. At last, we went home. Stanley brought out a jug of whiskey and poured himself and Tata a large glass. He and Tata sat in the kitchen as I heated water on the stove.

The girls came downstairs, but I chased them to bed, then set to work on Stanley's and Tata's cuts and bruises. Tata was bruised and bloody but that was all. I knew it pained him plenty as I washed the blood from his face and hair. A cut on Stanley's cheek needed seven stitches, but he never flinched once as I sewed. Their eyes glittering from whiskey and excitement, Tata and Stanley recounted the fight, blow by blow, toasting each other and themselves on the way they had torn into the Americans.

Their talk made me angry. "What kind of place is this America?" I cried. "Why would Americans do such a thing? Why do they hate us?" Then I looked at my father. "You and your America fever! Your letters never told me this about America. Your letters never told me many things."

Not waiting for Tata to answer, I took the lamp and left him and Stanley sitting at the kitchen table with their glasses of whiskey. Let them toast each other in darkness.

Monday, December 21, 1896

Jozef is disappointed that he missed a good fight, but I say, Too bad for him! He won't tell me where he was last night, and I don't like the way he smells, like tobacco.

The men have taken up a donation for repairs to Mrs. Wozniak's shanty. They have also rebuilt her table and chairs with scrap wood from the colliery.

Nobody knows who the Americans were, and Sheriff Martin says they may have been from out of town. The truth is, I don't think the sheriff is too worried about catching them and making them pay for the damages. Americans can vote. Foreigners can't.

Tuesday, December 22, 1896

A letter from Babcia and Stefania today! They sent me *Oplatek*, too. Stefania wrapped the wafer in a pretty manger scene that she drew herself. *Droga Swieta Anno!* I miss my grandmother and my best friend.

Thursday, December 24, 1896

It's Christmas Eve, and I have decided not to worry about Americans today.

There was much excitement as the girls and I prepared the *Wigilia*, the Holy Supper. Rose ground the mushrooms for the soup, and Violet mashed the potatoes while I rolled out the pierogi dough. I made three fillings — cabbage and mushrooms, sauerkraut, and farmer's cheese. By then Lily was feeling left out, so she helped me fill the pierogi. I fried them in butter and cooked extra of everything — potatoes, pierogi, soup, herring, bread.

All that cooking created a pile of dishes to wash, but I let them sit. I told the girls, "Let's pretend we are countesses who have maids to do the dishes."

I told them about Count Sadowski's manor house, and as we decorated the shanty for the Holy Supper, we pretended we had a grand manor house. We placed bundles of wheat and oats in the grand hall (actually the kitchen room) to ensure bread for the year to come. I covered the table with straw and told the girls how Jesus was born and laid in a manger. Then I spread out our coarse white cotton tablecloth, which we pretended was the finest linen, and we set our places. I set the blessed *Oplatek* on our best china (a dinner plate with only one small chip at the edge) in the middle of the table.

After our manor house was ready, we dragged the washtub in front of the kitchen stove, heated buckets of water, and had a bathing party. As I poured warm water over Rose's hair, she closed her eyes and said, "I'm thinking I want to call you Mama."

I hugged her, suds and all, and told her that was the best gift of all. So now Lily and Rose call me Mama. Violet won't, but that's fine with me. She has been less ornery these days, and I consider that gift enough from her.

I rinsed the girls' hair with tea, and we dried our hair in front of the stove. I set a lighted candle in the window and told the girls that we will eat when the first star of Christmas appears. Rose and Lily fought over whose job it would be to look for the star, but I hushed them and told them they will all look for it.

Now it is growing dark. Stanley will be home from work any minute. Tata and Jozef will come here, too, and they will bring a guest, to make sure we have an even number at dinner. It is bad luck to have an uneven number. Our seven dishes are cooked, the house is decorated, the table is set, the blessed wafer lies ready for Stanley to break, and the girls are dressed in their best clothing and watching at the window for the Christmas star. I have not forgotten a thing. I feel proud to have put my very first Christmas together.

I will write a letter to Babcia and tell her all about it.

SATURDAY, DECEMBER 26, 1896

I can hardly believe the guest Tata brought for Christmas dinner. Leon Nasevich! He works as a mule driver at the Honey Brook colliery. "It's the least I could do for a man from my old village," said Tata.

Stanley grew tight in the jaw the minute he saw Leon, and I could tell that amused Leon! I reminded Stanley to be a good host. If we turned Leon away, it would leave us with an uneven number, bad luck for sure.

So Stanley settled down and Leon stayed. Jozef insisted on sitting by Leon, and the girls took to Leon immediately, especially when he told them how animals kneel at midnight on Christmas Eve and talk in human voices. "Only the innocent at heart can hear them," he said.

After supper, Violet and Jozef went out to the cow shed to wait for the cow to talk. Leon commented on the stitches in Stanley's face and listened intently as Stanley and Tata recounted the fight. Then Leon talked about his union work, how on Saturdays he meets with mine workers, trying to get them to join the union.

It is easy to tell that Leon cares about the miners. He says they deserve more money and better working conditions. Stanley likes the idea of better wages and better working conditions, but he doesn't like the idea of union dues. Thirty cents a week is too much, and I agree. We can barely make ends meet now.

"Most miners waste far more than that on beer and whiskey," said Leon.

Oh, the scowl on Stanley's face!

At midnight, Leon went home, and we walked to the *Pasterka*, the Shepherd's Watch at St. Stanislaus's. I said an extra prayer for Leon, the sort of man who doesn't attend Mass, not even on Christmas.

SUNDAY, JANUARY 10, 1897

More snow. Mrs. Szarek gave me a sack of feathers, so my feather *pierzyna* is nearly done.

WEDNESDAY, JANUARY 13, 1897

Last night Stanley had a bad dream. He whimpered in his sleep, and it sounded as if he were crying. Then he said, *"Kocham cie*, Sophie." I lay awake the rest of the night, under our new *pierzyna*, feeling miserable and alone because he can say, "I love you" to Sophie but not to me.

TUESDAY, JANUARY 19, 1987

A cold, snowy day. Violet has a fever, so I kept her home from school. I made her tea with extra milk and sugar and wrapped her in the new *pierzyna*. All afternoon, we played school together. She likes to pretend to be the teacher, and I am her student. She shows me her schoolwork and teaches me what she has learned and makes me read and write on a slate. I am making good progress with my English, thanks to Violet. She likes it when I tell her that she is a good teacher.

THURSDAY, JANUARY 21, 1897

All three girls were sick yesterday. I cleaned up vomit and slop buckets until I felt sick to my stomach. I no sooner cleaned up one girl than the next one was crying.

Still, we needed bread. I mixed the bread dough and baked ten loaves. I shoveled a path to the outdoor bake oven and started a good-size wood fire. When the wood burned down, I swept out the ashes and put the loaves inside the oven to bake. I covered them with brown paper to keep the tops from getting too dark, then went inside to check the soup and the girls.

I must have left a few embers inside the oven because

soon I saw smoke. The papers had caught fire. I ran outside and yanked out the bread, but it was too late. The crusts were burned. "Papa's going to be mad," said Violet.

My stomach churned because I knew she was right. As the day wore on, I found myself growing feverish. By the time Stanley walked in the door, I was as sick as the girls and more irritable than a bear. Stanley took one look at the burned bread and hollered, "*Leniwa zona!* Do you think I work hard all day just so you can throw away good money?"

Maybe the fever caused me to snap. Or maybe it was the piled-up feelings I have had ever since the day we married. Or maybe I suddenly remembered that I was Anetka Kaminska, Mamusia's fiery redhead and Babcia's granddaughter who has *hart ∂ucha*.

I hollered back and informed him that I am not a lazy wife and that he should be more careful with the facts before he talks to me like that. I told him how sick the girls were all day and how sick I felt but that I had still tended them. I rattled off all the things I do each day — the cooking, the cleaning, the ironing, emptying slop pots, washing clothes, wiping noses and bottoms, and what thanks do I get? What an unlucky wife I am. I get a husband who says, *Kocham cie* to his dead wife in the middle of the night. Well, I can't be Sophie. I am Anetka.

At that, Stanley looked as senseless as if I had hit him

over the head. Lily started to cry and reached up for me to hold her. Rose clung to my skirt and sobbed, too. Violet stared wide-eyed at her father. "You said that?" she asked.

Her question jolted Stanley. He grabbed his coat and left. I put the girls to bed and washed their hot little faces with cool cloths and sang to them, then laid my head on Lily's pillow. The next thing I knew, it was morning. I went downstairs. Stanley was sitting at the kitchen table, blurry-eyed and reeking of beer.

SATURDAY, JANUARY 23, 1897

For the past few nights, Stanley has helped me put the girls to bed and hasn't yelled or criticized once. He kissed me afterward in bed last night. This morning, for the first time in our marriage, my heart feels happy, and I feel there may be hope for us. There's no marriage love yet, but I have been praying to Saint Ann that we will learn to be a good match.

FRIDAY, JANUARY 29, 1897

I will never know if Stanley and I could have grown into a good match. Four days ago I was wringing out the clothes when the Black Maria rumbled down our street. I crossed myself and ran to the window, praying that the wagon would continue past our house.

In the space of one Hail Mary, the wagon stopped in front of our shanty. I called on God, but *Moj Boze!* the driver climbed out and rapped on our door. I took my time drying my hands on my apron and even longer walking to the door, for the longer I took, the longer my husband was alive for me.

When I opened the door, the driver stood, his hat in his hand. He looked over my shoulder, then asked if Mrs. Gawrych, wife of Stanley Gawrych, was at home.

Yes, I nodded, yes, I am Stanley's wife. The driver blinked twice, no doubt because of my young age, looked over my shoulder again, saw Rose and Lily, then looked back at me. Then he said, "Stanley Gawrych died this morning in a roof fall."

At that moment, Rose came over to me, and began to whimper. I looked from her to Lily, who was twirling her hair and sucking her thumb, something she hadn't done in a long while. The room wavered snakelike around me, and I passed out cold.

The next thing I knew, Lidia was kneeling over me and the girls were sobbing. *"Moje dzieci!"* I cried. "My children!" They fell into my arms. "We will be all right. I am your Mamusia and I will take care of you, I promise." Lidia said she would take Rose and Lily down to her shanty and promised to get Violet from school.

By now, the driver and his helper had carried Stanley's body into the kitchen and set him on the floor. "Seems he should have put in an extra prop to hold up the roof," the driver explained. "Took three men all morning to dig him out, but he didn't suffer. Thought you'd want to know that."

Feeling numb, I climbed to my feet and went over to Stanley. He didn't suffer? How could he not have suffered? His back and legs were broken, and his neck was twisted. His face and body were bloody. The driver was halfway out the door when he said, "The company says you can stay on through winter. Company housing's for married men and families, you know."

No sooner had the driver left than Mrs. Szarek, Mrs. Wozniak, and Mrs. Mazur appeared at my door. They bossed me gently, telling me what to do. Mrs. Szarek helped me wash Stanley and get him ready for his wake. Other women came, their arms loaded with jars and breads and pies and other food, until the kitchen was more full than it had ever been when Stanley was alive.

As soon as Tata heard the news, he came. He asked if I wanted Stanley drained and filled with formaldehyde at the undertaker's, but I said no, that we would make do like in the old country. Tata reminded me that after three days, the body would smell, especially in winter when there were no flowers, but I assured him that Stanley would rest in peace easier, knowing that some money had been saved at his funeral. We would pack the body in ice.

Tata measured Stanley and rode into Hazleton to give the measurements to the undertaker. Before the day was over, Stanley was laid out in his funeral suit and resting in a plain pine coffin, set between two chairs.

Around sunset, everyone cleared out so I could have time alone with Stanley. I stood quietly by his coffin. He looked yellow in the light of the oil lamp, and his face was bruised and purple. I combed his hair again, gently, then wet my fingers and smoothed his eyebrows. Where was his miner's sense that day? Why hadn't he heard the crackling of the working roof? Why hadn't the rats warned him? Everyone knows the rats can sense things a man can't, and when the rats head up the slope, it means they sense a cave-in or explosion. Or maybe Stanley did hear. Maybe the rats did warn him. Maybe his tough Welsh foreman wouldn't let him leave.

No matter what had happened, it couldn't bring Stanley back. I told him I was sorry that he was dead and that I wished he had put the extra prop in, and I promised to watch over his little girls as best I could.

The wake began the next morning, and Father Dembinski was the first one at the door. Behind him stood a line of people who wanted to pay their last respects to Stanley and give their sympathy to me and the girls. They all wore sad, drawn, and respectful faces and said things like, I'm sorry about Stanley, or He was a good man, or He was a good worker. I knew I was supposed to find strength and comfort in their words, but they irritated me. I knew each man was glad it wasn't him lying there, and each woman was thankful it wasn't her husband — just as I had been each time before when the Black Maria came down the street.

Leon was there. His hair was brushed down hard and his face scrubbed clean. He moved through the slow line and stopped respectfully in front of Stanley's casket. Then he told me how sorry he was and shook my hand. I couldn't help myself. I moved into Leon's arms, and he held me. For a few minutes the scared feelings went away.

The room grew stuffy as it filled with people, women gossiping and passing around trays of food, men talking about the coal mines and their bosses and smoking pipes. At one point, I saw Leon with Violet, Rose, and Lily. He was squatting, talking to them at eye level. Violet left and returned with Buty. Leon scratched Buty on her head and under her chin. I could tell Buty liked that from the way she rubbed her head against his hand.

Mrs. Szarek and I sat up with Stanley's body. From time to time, she fell asleep, her head drooping against her chest. Even when I felt like sleeping, I couldn't. I kept thinking about the life Stanley and I were supposed to have, the match we were going to be, the babies we should have had, the father those little girls should still have, and I wondered why so many of my prayers are answered no.

I kissed Stanley, touched his hands, and crossed myself twenty-six times, once for each year of his life, then knelt and prayed for God to take Stanley into His kingdom. As I prayed, a strong feeling rose in my heart, until I felt as though my heart would burst, it felt so full. I was sure this sign was coming straight from God and that my prayer was answered yes. It felt good to know that God took Stanley in.

It fills me up each time I think about that feeling, and right now I'm so full of feeling that I can't write anymore. I will end here by saying that Father Dembinski said a beautiful funeral Mass, and now Stanley lies in the chapel at the cemetery, waiting for the ground to thaw enough for him to be buried.

WEDNESDAY, FEBRUARY 24, 1897

I wish that God would have more sympathy and understanding for someone in my position, a widow and mother to three little girls, and maybe, just maybe, make life easier for me, but no, God still makes His same jokes. He answers most prayers no and when He does answer yes, it may as well be no.

After Stanley's funeral, the company agent Mr. Bogdan

wasted no time in paying me a visit. He wore a new black suit with a bright blue tie, but I recognized him right away. He told me that Stanley owed a large debt to the company. I nearly fainted at the amount and asked to see the book. There, the black figure was inked beside Stanley's name, showing that he owed nearly $100 to the company store, including $44 for powder and $12 for smithing.

I burst out crying. *Droga Swieta Anno*, I prayed, how will I pay this debt? What will become of the girls and me? Sure, Tata and Jozef live with us, but their wages are barely enough to live on, let alone pay off such a large debt.

Saint Ann must have gotten through to God in a hurry, for in the next minute my prayer was answered. Without a blink or the offer of a handkerchief, Mr. Bogdan said, "If you are willing to work hard, I have three mine workers who need a place to board. That way, you can stay on as long as you like." He grinned broadly, showing his gapped front teeth. He was proud of his offer to help.

Three boarders. That means three dollars each month, plus money for food. With Tata and Jozef's help, it means enough to pay the rent and buy a few necessities. If I am thrifty, I can pay off Stanley's debt a little at a time. Right away I told Mr. Bogdan "Yes," and he said, "Good."

MONDAY, MARCH 1, 1897

Last night Mr. Bogdan introduced me to my three new boarders: Andrew Kaczmarek, a mountain of a man, and the Lasinski brothers, Marek and Artur.

From the doorway, I told the three men, "There will be rules around here. You'll get your clothes washed and your bathwater hot and ready at the end of each day. You'll get your meals cooked and your lunches packed. There will be no credit here or 'put on book.' You'll pay your board on time, you'll be on time for supper, you'll wash before you sit at my table, and there will be no liquor or disrespectful language or behavior in my house. I've got three young girls, and I intend to raise them right." How surprised I was to hear myself! I sounded as practical as Babcia.

Mr. Kaczmarek removed his hat and nodded respectfully at me. He elbowed the Lasinski brothers, and they did the same. The men moved their belongings into the loft where Tata and Jozef sleep. The girls sleep with me. Our bed is so crowded that we sleep crossways.

TUESDAY, MARCH 2, 1897

Wielki Post, the Great Lent, begins tomorrow. For the next forty days until Easter, we will give up meat and all things that come from flesh. No milk, cheese, eggs, or butter. I told the girls that we will know what it is like to be rich, since rich and poor alike renounce worldly things during Lent.

Rose said, "Mama, I feel sorry for the rich people. Lent will be harder for them. They are not used to fasting and giving up meat and good things to eat."

I thought about the Americans who live in the big white houses on Quality Road. Then I thought about all the times I had thinned the soup and fooled our stomachs with molasses for butter and potatoes for meat. "You're right," I told Rose. "Lent is nothing new for poor people like us."

WEDNESDAY, MARCH 3, 1897

Ash Wednesday. Twenty loaves of black bread sit cooling on my table. My arms ache from all that kneading! It is nearly noon, and already I have cracked coal, hauled water, and made the sour Lenten *zur* soup that Babcia always made.

As I mixed the coarsely ground rye, sugar, salt, garlic,

and water for the *zur*, I thought how, when I was a little girl, Lenten meals tasted awful but today I think only of the money I will save. My boarders pay the same for food each month, whether it's Lent or not.

FRIDAY, MARCH 5, 1897

I started a letter to Babcia, but I have not had time to finish it. I wanted to know whether the storks have returned to their nests yet, and whether it will soon be time to plow the fields.

In Sadowka I loved spring. It was a hopeful time when Babcia and I watched the sun move higher in the sky, when Mamusia and I waited for the great white storks, and when Jozef and I heard the ice break in the river. I loved to see the buds swelling on the trees, to smell the flowers and plants pushing through the dirt, and to hear the bees humming in the meadows.

But when the ground thaws here, Stanley will be buried, and there's no hope in that. I worry about Violet, who has nightmares and thrashes in her sleep. Rose whimpers and won't let me out of her sight. Lily sleeps, but she has started sucking her thumb again. At night she winds her fingers tightly around my hair, tugging so hard I fear I'll wake as bald as my boarder Artur Lasinski.

O Swieta Anno, I long to see the storks again, to kiss my grandmother, and to walk through the meadows with Stefania.

MONDAY, MARCH 8, 1897

A cold, cold day. It snowed four or five inches last night. Today as I was carrying an armload of wet clothes to hang from the rafters upstairs, I lost my footing and fell. I am sore but not hurt otherwise. How foolish I was not to watch where I was going! What if I had hurt myself? Broken an arm or leg? We have no money for a doctor, and who would care for the girls and the boarders?

WEDNESDAY, MARCH 10, 1897

I am in a foul mood! It is harder than I ever imagined to take care of four grown men, one brother, and three daughters. My hands are raw from doing so much wash and from picking coal in the cold. I have no time to comb my hair, and it has grown as tangled as a rat's nest. Today I gave up trying to work out the tangles, so I took a knife and chopped them out. Now I have three short patches. When Violet saw, she said, "Why didn't you use oil?" I don't know why I didn't remember the oil.

Thursday, March 11, 1897

This morning I was whisking around the kitchen, packing lunch pails, brewing coffee, cooking cereal, Mr. Kaczmarek came downstairs early and asked if we could talk. I said, "Sure, as long as I don't have to sit down, because I won't tolerate any man hollering that his breakfast isn't ready."

Mr. Kaczmarek acted nervous and fidgety. The way he kept clearing his throat made me suspicious. I kept one eye on my rolling pin in case I needed it fast.

Finally, he said, "Mrs. Gawrych, I am a hard worker and a strong man. It breaks my heart to see you working like a mule to take care of your girls. I understand your heartbreak because my father died when I was a boy. My mother did her best to raise us, but she worked herself to death. My brothers and I were sent to the orphanage. I don't want that to happen to you or your girls, so I will marry you if you say yes."

Marry me? I looked at Mr. Kaczmarek and saw nothing but kindness in his blue eyes. I know he meant every word, but as much as I like seeing kindness in a man, it isn't enough for a marriage. I thanked him and told him I am not afraid of hard work.

Since then, I have been thinking about the way Jerzy and Lidia look at each other, the way they are hungry for each other, and I know I will never marry again unless I love a man who loves me back. I'd rather live out my life as a widow, even if it means working myself into an early grave, which may be the best bit of rest I ever get.

The wind blew bitter cold, but I couldn't stand the shanty one more minute. After Violet left for school, I packed the mending and bundled up Rose and Lily, and we went across the patch to Lidia's. I was glad to find Lidia alone. Mrs. Wozniak had gone to Hazleton.

No matter how many times I see Lidia, I am touched all over again by what a good mother she is. I wonder what it would be like to be Lidia and to be married to a man like Jerzy.

Roman finished nursing. Lidia burped him, changed him, then put him down for his nap. Rose and Lily fell asleep, too, curled up together like kittens by the stove. Since it was Lent, Lidia poured hot water without tea into a cup for me. She looked at me and said gently, "How are you, Anetka?"

That's all it took for me to drop my sewing into my lap and let the truth spill out. "Mostly, I'm so tired that I could cry." Then I told her about Mr. Kaczmarek's marriage offer and how I had turned him down.

I expected Lidia to tell me I had done the right thing. To my surprise, she said, "Anetka, you are working yourself to death, can't you see that? You need to take care of your-self. How can you raise those girls alone? Pay your debts?"

"Are you saying I should marry the first man who comes along?" I said. "Are you forgetting that I am a widow?"

Lidia chided me gently. "The priest will give you dispensation. A widow in your position does not have to wait a year to take a husband when she has children."

Couldn't Lidia see? Did I have to point out the truth to her? Here I am, not even past my fourteenth namesake day, and I am a wife, a mother, and a widow.

"Why would I ever want to marry again?" I said. "My first marriage was not a good match. Stanley did not want a wife. He wanted a mother for his girls. I hate him for dying. I hate him for leaving such a large debt. I hate him for not loving me. I don't want or need another man to take care of. My house is crowded with men enough."

By the time I had finished saying all that, I was yelling and waving my arms and pacing. Rose and Lily woke up, wide-eyed and scared-looking. Lidia's mouth dropped open. I felt sorry that I had shocked her, but at that moment, I could not be like her, so full of goodness and gentleness, any more than I could make Stanley love me the way he loved his first wife or bring him back from the dead.

"I'm sorry," I said, but even my apology came out as a yell. Lidia looked as though she might cry. Then Roman cried. I had overstayed my welcome. I hurried the girls into their coats and stomped home. There, I banged pots and pans, kicked buckets, attacked the floor with the broom and swept like a mad woman, then stomped back to Lidia's. I hollered another apology at her front door, returned home, threw myself on the bed, and cried.

Droga Swieta Anno, please tell God if there's one thing I don't want, it's another man to take care of. I've had enough of marriage and men!

SATURDAY, MARCH 13, 1897

I am still in a foul mood. I hate cooking and baking and picking coal. I hate washing clothes and taking care of boarders. I hate my cold shanty and the cracks that the snow and icy wind blow through. But most of all, I hate Lattimer and the coal mines that make widows out of wives and orphans out of children.

MONDAY, MARCH 15, 1897

I have gotten in the habit of fetching the wash water on Sunday evenings for two reasons. One, so that I can get an early start on wash first thing Monday morning, and two, to avoid the sad looks I get from the women who gather at the well in the mornings.

It was growing dark last night when the girls and I carried the heavy buckets home. Violet complained that the buckets bruised her shins and wanted to know why boys never help carry the water, why it is always a girl's job.

I started to tell her that it is a girl's sacred duty and highest calling to learn to be a good wife and mother, but I stopped. I am starting to sound too much like Babcia! "You are right," I told Violet.

At that moment I heard a low moan coming from a ditch along the side of the road. It sounded like a man.

"Hurry to Lidia's," I told the girls, and they did. Cautiously, I walked over to the ditch and saw a man lying facedown.

"Mister," I said in English, kneeling by him.

His fingers moved feebly. Then he turned his head and whispered hoarsely in Polish, *"Pomoz mi."* "Help me," he was saying.

Moj Boze! It was Leon. I took off my coat and covered him, then ran home. Tata was sleeping off his whiskey, but Mr. Kaczmarek came with me. He crossed himself when he saw Leon. He carried Leon to the shanty as easily as if he were a sack of flour. I smoothed my *pierzyna* on the floor in front of the stove, and Mr. Kaczmarek laid Leon down gently. Oh, he looked terrible — all bruised and bloody — and I was glad the girls weren't home. Mr. Kaczmarek offered to clean Leon up. I said no, that there wasn't much left that could shock me anymore.

I got a pile of rags and heated water. Leon cracked

open his eyes, and his lids fluttered a few times. As I cut away his pants and shirt, all I could think was that the last time I washed a bruised and bloody man in my kitchen, he was dead.

TUESDAY, MARCH 16, 1897

For two days I have doctored Leon. I have thanked God over and over that Leon has no broken bones, just cuts and bruises and sore ribs and a large bump on his head. Most of the time he sleeps on the feather *pierzyna* by the coal stove and awakes only when I try to spoon soup into him. He awakes, too, when he needs the slop bucket and I have to help him. He hurts too much to know he should be embarrassed. The girls remember Leon from Christmas and their father's funeral, but they are timid around him. Jozef hopes Leon will board with us once he has recovered.

THURSDAY, MARCH 18, 1897

Today Leon is sitting up and able to get himself to the outhouse and back. He is wearing one of Stanley's old shirts and a pair of his pants, which are long in the sleeves and legs. His hair is cut short where I had to wash the nasty gash that ran from his crown to his right ear.

This morning he spoke for the first time. "We have a habit of bumping into each other," he said. Teasing lit his eyes for a second.

"Somebody else bumped you, not me," I said matter-of-factly. "Now, don't waste your strength talking when you should be eating." He tried to smile but grimaced instead. I spooned soup into him.

Leon ate, slept, then woke and ate some more. When he had strength enough, he told me what happened, slowly, as if each word hurt. My heart sank as he told me he was jumped by a group of Americans. They called him all sorts of bad names and told him to go back to where he came from, then they beat him senseless and left him for dead by the side of the road.

I felt the way I did in Sadowka when the Czar's soldiers pillaged the homes of my friends. "How can this happen here?" I said sadly. "We're supposed to be safe in America."

Leon didn't answer. He closed his eyes and fell back to sleep. As I sat there, watching him, I realized suddenly that God has played another joke on me. I told Saint Ann to tell God that the last thing I wanted was another man to take care of, and He sent Leon anyway.

Saturday, March 20, 1897

Payday. If Gomer Jones removed his hat, we would see two spiked horns! He has reduced the mine workers' wages, but the company still charges the same for food and rent.

I am glad that all my boarders pay on time. Tata and I have worked out a budget. He has never had a head for money, so he has agreed to put his wages and Jozef's wages in my hands, keeping only enough money for the beer wagon. Jozef fusses about handing over his pay envelope, but I have promised he can keep a nickel for himself each payday.

Sunday, March 21, 1897

Several American men and boys threw insults at us as we walked to Mass today. We watched our feet as we walked, careful not to look at their angry faces. I kept a close eye on Jozef, who has learned lots of English words to throw back.

Father Dembinski prayed for the coal company bosses and other Americans to open their hearts to the foreign mine workers and their families so that a strike can be avoided. I wonder if God will answer Father Dembinski's prayer yes or no.

WEDNESDAY, MARCH 24, 1897

Since Leon's beating, we have all grown more wary. We stay closer together and spend no more time alone than we have to. In the morning, the Polish, Italian, and Hungarian men gather outside my shanty and wait for Mr. Kaczmarek, who is so strong he drives a team of four mules. They think a big man like Mr. Kaczmarek can protect them. They go to and from work in a bunch, afraid to be found alone or in small groups. The strike talk is growing, which frightens Lidia. She says it's like throwing stones at a hornet's nest — no good can come from it.

MONDAY, APRIL 5, 1897

A few days ago, Father Dembinski told me the ground has thawed enough for Stanley to be buried, and now a common birch cross marks Stanley's grave. I kept Violet home from school, and the girls and I visited the cemetery. We knelt and prayed, and I told Stanley that I am taking good care of his girls and I told him again that I wished he had put an extra prop in that day. I can't help myself. I am still angry with him, even though it isn't right to stay angry at someone who is dead.

THURSDAY, APRIL 8, 1897

Although Leon has returned to work at the Honey Brook colliery, he still boards with us. I admit it feels handy to have him around. No matter how early I rise, he has already stoked the kitchen stove, fetched buckets of water, and has a full report to give me on the sunrise. We drink coffee together before the others come down. I like to hear him talk about work, about the pesky mules he drives in the Honey Brook colliery, the other miners, and the bosses. I also like to hear him whistling, and twice I caught him tickling Buty.

This morning Leon told me about one of his mules who refuses to work unless he gives her tobacco, which made me laugh. The mules are so clever that they know how many cars they are expected to pull and how many chambers they must visit. Don't ask a mule to pull an extra car or work an extra chamber, because she won't do it. "It's not in her contract," says Leon. "The mules are smarter than the men that way."

I looked at him sitting there, in his coveralls and shirt, thinking how he didn't look like a Czar's soldier anymore, just an ordinary man. Sometimes when Leon talks to Tata or Mr. Kaczmarek or the Lasinski brothers, he moves a certain way or speaks a certain way, more cautious and alert. I can see the soldier in him then. But never at my kitchen table.

SUNDAY APRIL 11, 1897

This morning I badgered Leon until he agreed to go to church, and then I was sorry. I don't know who is worse to mind: Leon or the children. First he got Rose and Violet giggling by crossing his eyes at them. Then Lily, seeing all the fun they were having, fussed because she wanted to sit on Leon's lap, not mine. She wiggled and squirmed, and I could not get her to sit still, but when she sat on Leon's lap, she was an angel. He made a smug, satisfied face at me as Lily snuggled against him, her thumb in her mouth.

I shot Leon a cross look, and he looked back at me, eyes wide, as if he hadn't done anything wrong. As soon as Mass ended, I scolded him for setting a bad example, especially on Palm Sunday, a most solemn day. It is hard enough for children to keep still during Mass without his antics.

"I'm sorry," he said, but I could tell from his eyes that he wasn't the least bit sorry for tormenting me.

Even though the girls have known him only a short while, they already side with him against me. Lily wrapped her arms around Leon's legs, and Rose said, "Don't be mad at Leon, Mama."

"I'm not mad," I said. "Now, let's get our palms." Leon grinned, no doubt pleased with himself. No matter how he tortures me, I always forgive him when I see how the girls have taken to him, even Violet. They miss their father, but they seem in better spirits around Leon. He never hollers or criticizes, and at night he's never too tired to play with them.

The sun felt warm and yellow as we walked home. Leon took turns carrying first Lily, then Rose, on his shoulders. He pretended to be a mule, and let the girls kick him and giddy-him-up and whoa and switch him with their palms. He whinnied and pawed the ground with his foot, which made even Violet laugh.

At home, I tucked the palms behind the crucifix and our holy pictures of the Blessed Mother and Jesus and Saint Ann to protect our house from lightning and fire. The last three I placed in my beehives the way Mamusia always did to ensure a good honey crop. "What a marvel bees are," said Leon.

At first my heart leaped to think that Leon knew bees in his heart. He poked about the bee boxes, then asked if I had ever seen the kind that have removable frames. A strange, cautious feeling crawled over me as I remembered how Stanley was interested in my beekeeping. I thought it was a good sign about Stanley, but it wasn't. My throat tightened and I changed the subject.

Good Friday, April 16, 1897

Jozef and his friends made an effigy of Judas from tattered clothing and stuffed it with straw, just like in Sadowka. They put thirty pieces of broken glass in Judas's pocket, dragged him through the streets, then threw him in the river.

Holy Saturday, April 17, 1897

I am sick of black bread, herring, and *zur*! This afternoon the priest blessed our Easter basket. Tonight I let the stove fire go out, the way Babcia always did on Easter eve. Tomorrow, the day of Christ's resurrection, I will start a new fire. Oh, the blessed eggs and juicy sausage and *Paska* bread we will eat tomorrow, Easter Sunday.

Tuesday, April 20, 1897

Easter has passed and the spring boss has arrived. While Violet was at school, Rose, Lily, and I spent the morning digging up the ground near the house, and the dirt and mud felt good. I have learned a lot from studying the gardens behind the Italians' shanties. The girls and I have planned the garden rows: We'll plant basil near the tomatoes and peppers, rosemary and oregano near the beans, and coriander and dill near the cabbage and carrots. And sunflowers, too. We will plant a whole row of sunflowers to guard our garden and grant good luck to the gardener.

THURSDAY, APRIL 22, 1897

The men's strike talk has reached the Pennsylvania government in Harrisburg. The governor has sent a committee to Hazleton to talk with the mine workers and their bosses. They want to find out if working and living conditions are as bad as the mine workers say. The committee met yesterday at the Central Hotel in Hazleton.

At dinner tonight, Leon called the committee a farce. He said the bosses have made sure that the committee questions only American mine workers who enjoy steady work and who will say what the bosses tell them to say. "How can such a committee learn about our living and working conditions from a hotel?" asked Leon. "Why don't they examine the mines?"

"They should shovel the coal," said Marek Lasinski.

"Psia krew!" said Mr. Kaczmarek. "They should drive four mules."

"They should pick the slate," said Jozef. "Then they'll know about red tips."

"They should eat our thin soup and see how many

ways they can fool their stomachs with potatoes," I said.

Only Tata thinks the committee will help us. "Things will get better," he said. "The governor has sent this committee."

FRIDAY, APRIL 23, 1897

The coal companies have called us undesirable foreigners!

Leon told us everything he had heard: "The coal bosses say we have no right to strike. They say no one is hungry in Lattimer and other coal patches. The bosses told the committee they fear we will attack the Americans if we don't get our own way. Now they say the government needs to send a cavalry troop to Hazleton to protect the Americans from undesirable foreigners like us. From us!"

Mr. Kaczmarek pounded the table with his fist. "The Americans are afraid we will attack them? Ridiculous! They attack us!"

"How can they call us undesirable?" said Jerzy. "We take the worst and most dangerous jobs, yet they pay us the least."

"Gomer Jones says he wants a full day's work for a full day's pay," said Marek Lasinski. "Well, that's what we want, too. A full day's pay for a full day's work. We want what every American wants."

"The problem is, we aren't Americans," said Tata.

Mr. Kaczmarek had something to say about that, but Leon stopped him with one look. Everyone grew quiet, the way they always do when Leon speaks. He isn't quick to make decisions like Tata. He never pounds a table with his fist or shouts to make himself heard like Mr. Kaczmarek. But when Leon speaks, he takes charge of the room and everyone in it.

"Anetka's father is right," said Leon, and that made Tata proud. "Some of us are Russian, some are Polish, and some are Lithuanian. Some of us are Slovak, some are Hungarian, and some are Italian. We speak our own languages and attend our own churches and practice our own traditions. The bosses can divide us, and if they can divide us, they can conquer us. We can't let that happen."

"I'd like to strangle them with my bare hands," said Mr. Kaczmarek.

"Violence isn't the answer," said Leon. "We need to stick together. We need to join the union."

At this, Lidia spoke up quietly. "Are you forgetting? The union is run by Americans. How can we trust Americans when it's Americans who cheat us, tax us, throw stones and insults at us? A union will only make the Americans hate us more."

"It's not possible for the Americans to hate us more," I said. "And that scares me more than any union."

Saturday, May 1, 1897

May Day is always full of surprises, and today Leon surprised me with a present. He told me to cover my eyes, and he led me out back then said, "Open your eyes." I was shocked to see a new bee box, the kind with the removable frames and a deep drawer for holding the honey.

"Well, what do you think?" asked Leon.

That strange feeling crawled over me again, the same feeling I had when Leon first asked me about bees. It reminded me of Stanley, and it made me nervous and angry at the same time. "*Nie chce.* I don't want it," I said. "You can keep it for yourself." I went back inside the house.

Sunday, May 2, 1897

I went to bed angry last night. This morning I untangled myself from Lily and slipped out of bed. I lit the kerosene lamp and tried to write in my diary, but the words wouldn't come, so I turned out the lamp and just sat.

Soon Leon came downstairs. He nodded at me to follow him outside, and I did. He took my hands and pulled me over to the new bee box. "Talk to me," he said.

My throat choked and I looked away so Leon wouldn't see me cry. He squeezed my hands tighter. I didn't want to tell him, but when he pulled me close, I leaned my head against his shoulder and sobbed. I couldn't help myself. Words and tears spilled out of me. I told Leon some things he knew already and some things he didn't know. I told him how scared I was to come to America, how scared I was to marry a man I didn't know and didn't love, how scared I was to raise three girls on my own, how I had hoped love would come for Stanley and me, how I thought Stanley's bee boxes were a good sign, but they weren't, and how it was just one more prayer that got answered no.

Leon stroked my hair. "Anetka," he said. *"Masz hart ducha.* You have a spirited heart. You are the bravest person I know." He tilted my chin so that I looked into his eyes and said, "Only a very courageous person continues to swim after she has lost sight of the shore."

He kissed the top of my head, and I felt that kiss tingle all the way down to my toes. He left me standing there and went inside the cow shed. I heard the cow low, eager to be milked. I heard Leon talk softly to her and to Buty, and I heard the clang of the milk bucket.

Hart ducha? He thinks I have a spirited heart? How can he think I am brave? What does he mean about swimming after I lost sight of the shore?

MONDAY, MAY 3, 1897

As soon as the dew dried this morning, the girls and I collected apple blossoms. I showed them how to snip sprigs from the tips of the branches. When our sack was full, we headed home to make scented oil from the apple blossoms.

Mrs. Wozniak and Lidia were outside, hanging clothes over the fence. Roman was lying on a blanket. I called hello to them both, and as Lidia turned, I saw that her belly was rounding out. "Lidia," I blurted out. "Are you expecting?"

She blushed and patted her belly. "September," she said.

"So soon!" I said and I hugged her.

As I walked home, I wondered again what it is like to be Lidia, to be loved like that. Even in her condition, she is still the prettiest woman. It must have something to do with her gentleness, her goodness, inside and out. A lonesome ache started inside me, and I found myself watching and waiting for Leon to come home and wishing I had somebody to love me.

TUESDAY, MAY 11, 1897

At the culm bank this morning, Mrs. Wozniak and Mrs. Szarek told me about a fire that destroyed the Jeansville breaker last night. The loss is estimated to be $75,000. The breaker was insured, but now five hundred men and boys are without work.

Mrs. Wozniak said that arson is suspected, and some people blame the mine workers, but that doesn't make sense to me. "Why would mine workers put themselves out of work?" I asked.

"It's not mine workers," said Mrs. Szarek. "It's ghosts." Then she told me about seventeen miners who drowned when the Jeansville mine flooded six years ago. Here's what happened: Two miners were blasting near an abandoned slope. Their maps said they were sixty feet away from the abandoned slope, but they were actually only five feet away. When the blast went off, it opened the old workings, and water poured through the hole. The two miners swam to safety, but seventeen others drowned.

Several days went by before rescuers could make their way through the flooded tunnels on a raft. They found a group of five miners, hungry but alive. Six more bodies were also found, so badly eaten by rats they were unrecognizable.

WEDNESDAY, MAY 19, 1897

I was slicing onions and cabbage for supper when the shanty door banged open. Violet hollered for me to come quick. *Moj Boze!* I prayed quickly. What sort of bad news now?

"What's the matter?" I said, wiping my hands on my apron. "What has happened?"

"Bees!" said Violet. "They're swarming!" Excitedly, she told me how she had heard a low hum as she walked down the schoolhouse lane. Before her eyes, a cloud of bees hovered for a moment in the air, then gathered like a huge pinecone at the end of a sapling branch.

I left the cabbage and onions lying in a heap on the table. I grabbed a burlap sack and a sharp knife and followed Violet to the sapling. Violet held the burlap sack as I cut the thin branch, and the entire swarm dropped into the sack. I tied it up, carried it home, and dumped the swarm like a bushel of beans onto a cloth spread in front of my new bee box.

The queen lay in the center of the swarm, beautiful and confused. I snatched her and stuck her inside the hive. Within seconds the bees realized their queen was missing. Three bees approached the hive, then signaled the others by raising their tails high and fanning their wings. The rest of the bees poured into the hive.

Oh, the joy on Violet's face! She knows bees in her heart!

Friday, May 28, 1897

All four bee boxes are filled with busy boarders. After supper, I wrote a letter to Babcia, asking her about my hives in Sadowka. I asked her to please make sure that the grass is cut around the bee boxes and that the entrances are clean and to make sure that no mice have made their nests inside.

Sunday, May 30, 1897

Last night we sat up late on Mrs. Szarek's porch, talking about the new alien tax law. After July 2, every employer will be taxed 3 percent for each worker who is not an American citizen. The employers will deduct the tax from the workers' pay.

"We must hurry up and become citizens," said Tata. "We must take out our 'first papers.'"

"That's another reason the Americans hate us so," said Mr. Kaczmarek. "They don't want us to become citizens. That means we could vote."

Leon thinks the new alien tax law may help unite the foreign workers. He says the new law will make the foreigners see that they all suffer the same terrible working conditions, no matter what language they speak, what traditions they practice, what church they attend. He says the immigrants will see the value of a union such as the United Mine Workers. And if the bosses won't listen, he says, a strike is the only way to make them learn what is fair.

Lidia looked to Jerzy for comfort, and he squeezed her hand. Each time Lidia hears the word *strike,* she shudders. Even if I do have *hart ducha,* when I look at Violet, Rose, and Lily, the idea of a strike scares me, too. I hope and pray Leon is right.

TUESDAY, JUNE 1, 1897

Tata came home today, smelling like too much beer. He waved papers in his hand. They are *first papers,* his declaration of intent to become an American citizen. He said the Hazleton court office was crowded with foreigners, all taking out first and second citizenship papers.

Oh, Tata is proud of his papers. He hugged them to his chest and said that in two years, he can get his *second papers.* "All I need are two good American witnesses to tell the court I am a good man," he told us. "Then I take a test and become an American citizen."

"Two good Americans!" said Mr. Kaczmarek. "Where will you find them?" He and the Lasinski brothers laughed. Tata looked confused at first, not understanding the joke. Then he laughed, too.

I didn't see anything worth laughing at. I can't help but feel sad when I see Tata's papers. A year has passed since we left Sadowka, but I still feel the heartbreak of missing Babcia.

Friday, June 4, 1897

As I carried the milk pail to the house this morning, I saw Leon stoking the stove. I stood in the doorway, watching him. Sometimes I see the same arrogant soldier I knew in Sadowka, but I also see much kindness that pleases me. After he left for work, I found myself humming and thinking about his kisses.

Sunday, June 6, 1897

O Swieta Anno! The next time I find myself thinking about Leon's kisses, I will drop to my knees and recite the Rosary.

On our way home from Mass today, we saw bicycle riders. Most are American men and women, but a few foreigners own bicycles, too. The bicycle amazes me for a few reasons. First, I cannot imagine how a person does not topple over. Second, I cannot imagine spending hard-earned money on a bicycle.

"Would you ever buy one," I asked Leon, "if you had the money?"

Leon looked at me in a way that made me wish he would kiss me. "I am saving my money for something more important than a bicycle," he said.

"What might that be?" I asked.

He leaned so close that my knees trembled. "Union dues," he whispered.

O, on jest trudny! He is impossible!

WEDNESDAY, JUNE 9, 1897

No boss is hated more than Gomer Jones. Last night Mr. Kaczmarek said Gomer Jones found more black crepe tied to his door and more threatening letters. "Someone even tried to blow up his house in Audenreid," he said happily.

"Who?" I asked.

"Some say the Italians," said Mr. Kaczmarek. "Some say Hungarians. Some say Lithuanians. Some say Poles. Everyone wants the credit."

SATURDAY, JUNE 19, 1897

Payday. Tata and the others paid their board on time. How glad I was to put five dollars toward my debt at the company store. That leaves eighty-seven dollars left to pay. Soon the honey flow will begin and that will mean even more money.

MONDAY, JUNE 21, 1897

Lidia isn't the only one losing her shape to motherhood. Buty's belly is swollen, too.

SATURDAY, JUNE 26, 1897

The honey flow has begun. Violet and I collected fifty pounds of honeycomb from my new bee box, much more than I got from the old-fashioned ones.

TUESDAY, JUNE 29, 1897

The trouble with Americans has died down, so today after I filled a basket with jars of apple-scented cream, Violet and I walked to Hazleton. When Miss Mackinder heard the bell on the shop door jingle, she practically ran to greet me. My English has grown much better since last summer, and I felt pleased that I was able to make myself understood. I left her shop with nearly two dollars and an order for more cream.

All the way home I wished that all Americans were as kind as Miss Mackinder. When Violet and I reached the large gum tree, where the road forks into Quality Road and Main Street, five American boys were throwing rocks at a black cat. It was Buty! Before I could grab Violet, she ran after them and hollered in English, "Stop it!"

The cat darted across the street. "Stop it," they called, mocking a girl's voice. "Stop it! Stop it!" They pelted us with stones and called us "Hunky" and other names.

I hugged Violet close to me. "Walk fast," I said. "Keep your head down."

The boys hollered more insults and threw more stones. I shielded her as best I could. A stone hit my leg and another my shoulder. Then one struck Violet above her eye. She cried out, and I saw she was bleeding.

I know how a mother cat feels when she puffs herself up twice her size to defend her kittens. I screamed and ran at the boys like a wild woman. Their eyes popped out like frogs' and their mouths dropped open as though they were trying to catch flies. They dropped their stones and ran.

"Mama," said Violet, "you are brave."

She called me Mama! "So are you," I said, kissing her forehead. "So are you."

At home, I washed and bandaged Violet's cut. As soon

as Jozef saw the bandage, he said *"Psia krew!"* and he demanded to know whether Violet was all right, which surprised me since all those two do is squabble. She is more hurt inside than outside, and she has been fussing about Buty. Jozef said he will look for the cat, that he isn't afraid of American boys.

WEDNESDAY, JUNE 30, 1897

Jozef came home wet today. He smelled oily, like the brown water that fills the holes in the coal strippings. I don't know what to do about my brother, who has been swimming when he should have been working.

THURSDAY, JULY 1, 1897

Every night, Violet bangs on Buty's dish and calls for her, but so far, no luck. My brother has a black eye, and his knuckles and knees are scraped and bloody. "The American boys look worse," he said. That's all he would say.

Sunday, July 4, 1897

A year ago today I met Stanley Gawrych.

After Mass, Leon took the girls to watch a baseball game, so I could visit Stanley's grave by myself. As I knelt by the plain birch cross, I prayed, then told Stanley how big the girls are growing. I told him that Lily has stopped sucking her thumb, that Rose doesn't cry anymore at night, and that Violet has bees in her heart. I told him that I'm doing my best to raise them right and that I'm not mad at him anymore.

Wednesday, July 9, 1897

Tonight as I milked the cow, I heard a loud, contented purring and saw Buty lying in the straw. She lay there, watching me through slitted eyes. Three black kittens nursed at her belly.

"Violet," I called from the doorway. "Rose! Lily! Come quick!"

The girls squealed like tickled mice at the sight of the kittens. "Can we keep them?" asked Violet.

"Oh, yes," I said. That's one good thing about being grown-up: I can keep as many kittens as I want!

Friday, July 16, 1897

More mine workers seem to be taking matters into their own hands. Last night, at the Hazle Company breaker, the night watchman discovered a fire set at the blacksmith shop. He fired a shot at a man running from a lokie, a coal locomotive, but luckily the man escaped. The watchman extinguished the fire, and now authorities are searching for the culprit.

Saturday, July 17, 1897

Payday. We hoped that the alien tax would not be withheld from the mine workers' pay envelopes, but our hopes were dashed. Every unnaturalized worker's pay was docked 3 percent. Leon said if the tax means that much to the bosses, it means even more to the workers. Even though there was a hardness to Leon's voice that made everyone sit up and pay attention, I found myself thinking about his mouth and its kisses. I haven't been kissed in a very long time.

Friday, July 23, 1897

Jozef and his friends skipped work today and hopped a train to Wilkes-Barre to see the hanging of "Terrible Pete" Wassil, who murdered a man last year. Officers were stationed outside the jail to keep anyone from getting close, and the boys watched from the hill behind the jail.

They came home with gruesome details. After Sheriff James Martin placed the noose around Terrible Pete's neck and a black cape over his face, he pulled the rope that released the trap door. Terrible Pete dropped, his neck broken. It took twelve minutes for him to die, but his body was left hanging a full twenty-eight minutes.

My brother is a difficult, troublesome boy, but I could see that he was terribly bothered by the execution of this man and by the sort of man who could tie a noose.

Thursday, August 5, 1897

I don't feel safe until Leon comes home at night. I storm around the shanty, keeping busy, afraid to stop because stopping only makes me think and worry that Leon may be lying in a ditch somewhere. When he does get home, he's exhausted. It's hard for him to go to the mines at six, work all day, then spend hours at night talking up the union. Tonight he told Jozef that the breaker boys should join the union too, just like the men. They would hold their own junior meetings and vote at the men's meetings when policy was being decided. Leon said that the boys are just as important as the men. Without the breaker boys, the company can't process the coal for market. Jozef likes the idea, and now I have one more thing to worry about.

WEDNESDAY, AUGUST 11, 1897

Gomer Jones is a low-down, belly-crawling snake. He has already trimmed as much as he can from the wages of the miners and their butties. Now he has found a way to get more work out of the mule drivers and their mules with no additional pay.

He has created one central mule stable for five collieries. Instead of being stabled at each mine, the mules live together in one big stable. This way, the company needs only one crew to feed, water, and care for the mules. The coal company will save money on labor, pasturing, facilities, and deliveries.

Leon and the other Honey Brook mule drivers do not like the new system. With one central stable, the drivers will have to walk farther to get their mules each morning. For many drivers, it means an additional hour each morning and each night, yet no additional pay, since the drivers aren't paid until the mules are in the mines. They complained to Gomer Jones, but he doesn't care.

Friday, August 13, 1897

For the past few days, Leon and the other Honey Brook drivers have retrieved their mules from the central stable. The walk makes the drivers angrier and angrier each day, because they are working two extra hours with no extra pay. Yesterday they asked Gomer Jones for a raise, but he refused, saying it's not his problem. Now Leon and the other Honey Brook mule drivers have called for a strike tomorrow.

Lidia's troubled face told me she is worried that the strike might spread to Lattimer, where Jerzy works. Hugging little Roman closer, she said, "We don't need the trouble."

"We must seize our opportunity," said Leon. "How many more injustices must we suffer? How many more women and children must suffer because of greedy coal bosses?" He rested his hand on my shoulder, and it felt strong and sure. "Think of Anetka and Mrs. Wozniak, how they lost their husbands and have no pension or insurance. Think of last year's Twin Shaft disaster in Pittston and all the fatherless children." He went on to cite numbers he had learned at a union meeting. "Just last year, there were nearly 2,000 accidents. Nearly 500 men and boys died. They left 200 widows and 600 fatherless children."

"What will we live on if the men strike?" said Lidia. "We need the money."

I lifted my chin. "Jones has fired too many men who also need the money. He has cut the wages of others who need the money. He needs to learn how to treat us, and a strike is the only way to teach him and the other bosses."

Leon gave me a look that I read with my insides, not my eyes. He was proud of me, I could tell.

"Maybe the bosses do need a lesson," said Lidia. "But such lessons have a price, and someone must pay." Roman started to fuss in her lap, and Lidia left our shanty to nurse the baby in private.

SATURDAY, AUGUST 14, 1897

This is how Leon tells the story of Gomer Jones and the crowbar. Leon and thirty-five other Honey Brook mule drivers formed a picket line this morning. They blocked the entrance to the colliery to keep other miners from going to work.

When Jones came out of his supervisor's shed, he took one look at the strikers and went back inside. "He's scared of us," said a driver. "He's hiding."

Jones wasn't hiding. He came out wielding a crowbar. He approached the mule drivers, grabbed the youngest boy, and began to beat him. The boy wrestled the crowbar away from Jones and turned it on him. The mule drivers jumped in, grabbing Jones's arms. They threw him to the ground. Another driver grabbed a rock, ready to dash in Jones's head. Luckily for Jones, he was saved by another supervisor, who rushed over and pulled him to safety.

The strikers raced to the breaker whistle tower and blew the signal for work to stop. The breaker boys streamed out of the breaker, cheering. Men poured from the slag heaps, the outbuildings, the mines. As the men and boys hurried home, they told everyone they met about Gomer Jones and his crowbar.

SUNDAY, AUGUST 15, 1897

I have taken the oil lamp and am lying across the bed with the girls. As I left the kitchen, Leon saw my diary, grinned at me, and said, "Make sure you write something about me." Oh, isn't he the most conceited man!

It's late. Every time I close my eyes, I hear Leon's low voice, rising and falling like a lullaby, as he talks with the men gathered in our shanty. They are talking about the new alien tax, the strike, and the things they'd like to do to Gomer Jones and men like him who hate foreigners.

"*Psia krew!*" said Tata. "I have lived in America for over two years now, and I am learning English and American ways. I have my first papers, and soon I will be an American, too."

Mr. Kaczmarek laughed. "Papers don't matter. You're a foreigner and always will be to them."

"That's the one thing all foreigners have in common," said a Lasinski brother. "No matter what country they're from."

"That's why we must act together," said Leon. "Individually, we can be fired and blacklisted or worse. But together, we can win."

Droga Swieta Anno! Let Leon be right!

Tuesday, August 17, 1897

Yesterday, the Honey Brook strikers walked from breaker to breaker, patch village to patch village throughout the Hazleton area, persuading other mine workers to strike. So far the Lattimer breakers are still running. Leon says it's just a matter of time before the strike reaches us. Already the strike has grown to nearly three thousand men! Nearly all the strikers are foreigners, and that concerns Leon. He wishes the American workers would see that they, too, would benefit from a strike.

"Why should they strike?" said Mr. Kaczmarek. "They have the best jobs and the highest wages."

"Wait and see," said Leon. "When the Americans have no foreigners to take the worst jobs, then the worst jobs will fall to Americans."

I know the strikers' grievances by heart: They want Gomer Jones fired, their previous wages restored, raises for the men who work underground, an end to the company store system, and the cost of blasting powder reduced from $2.75 a keg to $1.50. They also want each and every striker to be reinstated after the strike.

The general mine superintendent has fired bosses and clerks who sympathize with the strikers, and he has sent Coal and Iron Police squads to patrol the patch villages where the strikers live. He refuses to negotiate with the strikers until they have returned to work.

WEDNESDAY, AUGUST 18, 1897

Gomer Jones has been arrested and charged with aggravated assault and battery. Tomorrow there will be a big meeting of the striking mine workers. They will listen to speeches given by the district president of the United Mine Workers.

Thursday, August 19, 1897

Over a thousand mine workers sat in the hot sun on the Honey Brook baseball grounds and listened to speeches given by John Fahy. Mr. Fahy sounds a lot like Leon. He urged the men and boys not to turn to violence. If they use violence, he said, it will hurl the strikers headlong into a conflict that they cannot win. He also told them they need a union that will work for them and help them negotiate with the coal companies. But he doesn't want to force anyone to join the United Mine Workers. The men need to join on their own. Last, he reminded the mine workers that he is not in favor of a strike. A strike is a last resort, used only when negotiations have failed.

Saturday, August 21, 1897

Payday. Again, the alien tax has been withheld. The mine owners are not willing to negotiate. They say we are greedy, but the truth is, I have never met a greedy mine worker. I only know men who want food for their families, clothes and shoes for their children, a decent house, money to pay a doctor, and some left over for the beer wagon.

Tonight Italians, Hungarians, and Poles are going

from house to house, from patch to patch, to spread word of the strike.

Mr. Kaczmarek has bought a gun. He wants to be prepared if the strike comes to Lattimer. This upset Leon, who says they must prepare peacefully. "No striker should carry a gun. No knives. No clubs. Even one drop of blood is too much."

"*Psia krew!*" said Mr. Kaczmarek. "You mean we should let the Americans blow us away, even though it's their fault in the first place?"

"We will arm ourselves with the American flag," said Tata.

Leon agreed. "A flag will show that we want the same for our families as every American man wants for his."

"You think a flag will protect you?" said Lidia, her voice shrill. "You think it will shield bullets?"

Friday, September 3, 1897

Tonight I was drying and putting away the dishes when Leon came home. I saved him some supper, but he was too fired up to eat. He told me about one thousand striking mine workers who marched from McAdoo to Hazleton.

He told me how the strikers won their day. They carried American flags and the red socialist flags. People joined them along the way, and by the time they reached Hazleton, the parade numbered over three thousand. Shopkeepers watched from their doorways, and citizens watched from their windows.

In all, the strikers marched eleven miles and shut down four collieries. When Leon tells me all this, I see a fire burning inside him, but I feel only darkness growing inside me. I am scared, though I try not to show it.

Monday, September 6, 1897

Leon came home late tonight. I hate it when he's late! I feel spooked by every shadow and I jump at every noise outside. I can't even go to the outhouse without watching over my shoulder. Mrs. Szarek tells Lidia and me to go about our days as usual, but how can I pick mushrooms and coal, do wash, bake bread, and walk Violet to school when I am scared? O Saint Ann, why must those Americans hate us so?

Tuesday, September 7, 1897

Last night, I tossed and turned and had a dream too frightful to write. Today I have felt a deep sadness all day.

I hear the two Lattimer breakers running, and I wonder how long they will run before the strike reaches us. Leon says that Lattimer must strike, too, that everyone must stick together. I know he's right, but I am praying that the strike doesn't come here, that it will be over soon.

Some strikers are using force to persuade their fellow workers to join them. In a nearby village, strikers have thrown stones through windows and dynamited the shanties of those who haven't joined the strike.

WEDNESDAY, SEPTEMBER 8, 1897

I have never had cross words with Lidia, but yesterday we argued about the strike and how all the patch villages must stick together. She broke down and cried. "Don't you see?" she said. "I don't want the strike to come here. I am not strong like you."

O Swieta Anno! Didn't Lidia know? I may sound brave on the outside, but inside I tremble like a newborn calf. "The truth is that all this talk about unions and strikes scares me, too," I told her. "I do not feel safe at night until Leon is home."

She looked at me, surprised, and suddenly we weren't talking about the strike anymore. "You love him," she said. "You love Leon, don't you?"

"No," I stammered. "I don't love Leon. How can you think I love him? He torments me and he laughs when I get angry. He doesn't go to Mass regularly and, when he does go, he pokes me and gets the girls giggling. I have never seen him pray."

I didn't tell her about the way he kissed me on the boat, when he knew very well I was betrothed, and then again at my wedding, but inside my head I added those reasons. "No, there is too much about Leon that my head tells me to feel cautious about."

"What does your heart tell you?" asked Lidia. When I didn't answer, she said, "That's the miracle of love — that when there are so many reasons not to love someone, we still love."

Roman started to fuss, and Lidia lifted her blouse to nurse him. He suckled like a noisy horse! We both laughed at that, and I said, "Soon you'll be nursing two babies."

She smiled and said, "Life is full of unexpected surprises, isn't it?"

Then Lidia put my hand on her stomach and let me feel the baby. Just as I was wondering whether I was patting the baby's head or bottom, the baby kicked me right in the hand! "What a wonderful thing it must be to have a baby growing inside you," I said to Lidia.

She grew teary-eyed and nodded. Then we talked about Roman's new tooth and the way he says, "Ma-mama-ma." All my cross feelings disappeared. I was glad the subject had changed from Leon, even though I still thought about him between each and every word. I wonder if Lidia is right about love.

FRIDAY, SEPTEMBER 10, 1897

This morning Leon hung back after Tata and the other boarders went to work. Leon was dressed in his best white shirt and black stovepipe pants. It wasn't the day to bake bread, but I needed to keep my hands busy, so I got out the wooden tub that I use to knead dough.

Leon dragged the heavy sack of rye flour over to the table and said, "We're marching from Harwood to Lattimer today. I think we can persuade Lattimer to turn out. They said they will if they are called out."

I knew I should be brave, but I couldn't be. "So let them come," I said. "You don't have to go with them."

He shook his head and said, "You know I do."

I started dumping flour into the bin, not saying a word. Leon touched my chin and I looked up at him. Suddenly, his lips were on mine. Something inside me burned as if I were on fire. I moved into his arms, and as I did, I knocked over a tin of flour, scattering it over the table and floor.

He touched my cheek with his finger where I knew a tear was trailing, then put his hand on my heart. "*Masz hart ∂ucha,"* he said. Then he stepped away, and I saw the flour streaked his pants. He touched his hat good-bye and slipped out the door, where Jerzy stood waiting. A terrible feeling of dread hung over me.

O Swieta Anno! I do love that man, no matter what my head says.

LATER

I could have just swept up the spilled flour, but I needed to keep busy or feared I would lose my mind. So after the bread was baked, I scrubbed the floor on my hands and knees. The breaker whistle blew. *Moj Boze!* My heart turned over, the way it did my first day in Lattimer, when Jozef and I waited for Tata on Mrs. Szarek's porch.

It was too early for work to be over, so the breaker whistle could mean only one thing: warning! I hurried to the doorway and looked toward the breaker.

A few minutes later, Violet burst through the door. "Mama," said Violet, "the sheriff and his deputies are in Lattimer. They have guns. The strikers are marching over the hill."

"Guns?"

I crossed myself and prayed harder than ever before. In the middle of my fifth Hail Mary, I heard a splintering sound like the snap of dry wood. Gunfire. I don't remember how long the shooting lasted, maybe a minute, maybe two, maybe five. I'll never forget the sudden silence when it stopped.

"Watch your sisters," I told Violet. "Stay inside and away from the windows."

I picked up my skirt and ran as fast as I could, barefoot, up the winding dirt path. Other women were running, too, their head kerchiefs trailing like shadows behind them. When we reached the schoolhouse lane, we shrieked at what we saw. Bleeding strikers lay sprawled near the trolley tracks and across the grass and up the hillside and near the large gumberry tree. Others lay in a ditch, some already dead and some dying. Everywhere, men groaned and screamed and cried for water. The smell of gunpowder hung in the air.

I could only think of finding Leon. I stepped around two men who had been shot in the back and around another man who clutched his stomach. Blood poured through his fingers. A boy was crying for help for his shattered knees. Another was shot twice in the forehead.

People came out of their houses. Some carried water and some were tearing sheets into bandages. I saw Violet's teacher, holding the hand of a dying man. It was then that I realized that not one of the dead, dying, or wounded men and boys had a gun. They were all unarmed, shot down like dogs.

Droga Swieta Anno! Where was Leon? Was he all right?

I searched near the trolley tracks, the schoolhouse, the gumberry tree. The minutes stretched by. More people came to help and ambulance wagons and drays came up the road from Hazleton.

Two men came along and lifted a man onto a stretcher. They carried him to a wagon and slid him inside with three other moaning men. I ran to look, but none was Leon. The driver clucked his tongue, and the horses started off, pulling the wagon toward Hazleton.

It grew hard to make sense of the people and things around me, but I spotted Mrs. Szarek and Mrs. Wozniak tending a wounded man. Then I saw Lidia. She was cradling Jerzy's head. His eyes were staring, and I knew he was dead. "Oh, my Jerzy," she cried.

I ran to Lidia and put my arm around her, but she didn't know I was there. At that moment, the trolley rolled past, and I saw Sheriff Martin and his deputies. Some were laughing and pointing as they looked at the bodies lying in the street.

Somehow, Mrs. Wozniak and I got Lidia home to bed, then I went back to help the wounded as best I could. I am home now, sitting at the table. *O jej!* I am angry. I am angry that four hundred men and boys marched to Lattimer this afternoon. I am angry because at last count, fifteen men and boys are dead and at least thirty-two more are wounded, and who knows how many more? I am angry because I don't know if Leon is dead or alive and I am afraid that God might have taken him the way He took Mamusia and Stanley and Jerzy.

I didn't want Leon to march today, but he did, even though he knew how I felt, and that makes me so angry that if he were to walk through the door this minute, I would yell at him and tell him what an impossible man he is.

SATURDAY, SEPTEMBER 11, 1897

The girls are so frightened and exhausted. Last night they cried themselves out, then fell asleep in my arms. Tata and Mr. Kaczmarek carried them to bed.

As for me, I stormed around the kitchen, sweeping the floor, banging pots and pans, kicking buckets and chairs. I scared everyone — Tata, Mr. Kaczmarek, the Lasinski brothers, and Jozef. They think I am a madwoman. Well, I am. I am madder than I have ever been in my whole life. I am mad at Leon, at the Sheriff and his men, and at God, who never seems to answer yes to any of my prayers.

At last I couldn't clean or kick anymore. I collapsed into bed but slept fitfully and had frightful dreams. When I awoke, it was time to get ready for Jerzy's funeral, which Lidia held privately at Mrs. Wozniak's. Lidia looked like a ghost of a person, but all through the funeral she sat and spoke gently and politely, never breaking down or crying. She seemed to find comfort and strength in the words of the priest and the mourners.

Lidia has always been like that, full of love and goodness, and taking care of others before herself. After the funeral, I asked her what she intends to do. "As soon as this baby is born," she told me, "I am taking my children home to Poland. I have had enough of America."

"Where will you live?"

"If my parents don't take me in, Jerzy's will," she said, her voice shaking. Then she looked at me, concerned. "What about you? Has Leon —"

My chin trembled. "I don't know where he is, whether he's lying hurt someplace or —"

Lidia squeezed my hand. "I pray he comes home safely to you."

Oh, Lidia, gentle, kind, forgiving, accepting Lidia, to care about me when she has so many troubles of her own. I reached for her, and we fell into each other's arms, crying.

Sunday, September 12, 1897

The girls and I dressed for Mass, the same as we do every Sunday, but when we got outside the church, my feet stopped. I could not bring my legs to move. I know Babcia would tell me to go to Mass and pray, but my heart told me, What good is prayer when so many prayers get answered no?

Droga Swieta Anno! I knew it wasn't right to feel that way, but I did. I would never, could never be like Lidia. The girls didn't understand. "Come on, Mama," said Rose, tugging my arm. "We're going to be late."

"No, we're not," I said. "We're going home."

Violet looked as though she thought lightning might strike me dead, but my mind was made up. I was listening to my heart, and my heart said, "Go home." So I did.

I changed out of my clothes and set about dinner. I decided we would eat the lazy chicken that only lays one egg a week. She squawked as I grabbed her by the tail feathers and struggled as I carried her over to the chopping block, where I stretched out her neck. As I raised my hatchet she stopped struggling and just lay there, her beady eyes watching me. I looked at that helpless chicken, and I couldn't do it. I let her go, saying, "Shoo! Go on! Get out of here!"

The chicken ruffled her feathers and flapped her wings twice. I wrapped my arms around myself and sank to my knees. Crying and shaking all over, I yelled up to God. I told him how selfish it was to take Jerzy from Lidia, Stanley from his girls, and Mamusia and Leon from me. I told Him that I want to believe in prayer but sometimes I need a prayer to be answered yes to help me through the hard times, and is it too much to ask for a sign?

I knew I shouldn't talk to God that way, but I couldn't help myself. There was more I wanted to say when I caught sight of a man walking unsteadily up the lane. He had a bloody bandage wrapped around his shoulder and chest.

I blinked and wiped my face. "Leon?" I said, climbing to my feet. "Leon!" In that second, I forgot what an impossible man he is and how angry I was at him. I ran and leaned my face into his neck and held on for dear life.

He circled his arm around me, wobbling slightly. "You feel good," he said, leaning heavily against me.

"Let me help you inside," I said.

"Anetka —"

"Hush," I told him, putting my finger to his lips. "There's plenty of time to talk later, when you're stronger."

I helped him into the shanty and into bed. As he leaned back against the pillow, he touched my face with his hand and said, "You're crying."

He grinned, ever so slightly but still teasing, and said, "I always liked it when you cried. It gave me an excuse to hold you."

I sniffled and wiped my cheeks. "Leon Nasevich, you are an impossible man —"

"I am," he said. "Anetka, I love you." He fell asleep, and I laid my head next to his on the pillow and cried more tears than I ever knew I had.

Oh, my heart hurts for Lidia, especially when I think how I had envied her and longed to have what she had with Jerzy. Now I am the one to know good fortune while she knows sorrow. How quickly our lives can change forever. Over and over I have thanked God that Leon is alive.

Saint Ann, I may never understand all of your signs and God's workings, but I do know this: Some prayers do get answered yes after all.

EPILOGUE

Two months after the Lattimer massacre, Anetka and Leon were married. Leon continued to work as a union leader for the United Mine Workers of America. Although Anetka supported his union work, she never felt safe until he was home at night. Anetka and Leon wanted a houseful of children, but they only had one daughter, Mary.

Anetka added twenty more beehives. She continued to make balm for Miss Ada Mackinder. Miss Mackinder sold the balm in fancy jars to some of the wealthiest women in Hazleton. Anetka laughed to herself when she wondered what the American women would think if they knew it was bag balm.

Stanley's three daughters grew to love Leon. Violet and Jozef never did marry, despite Mrs. Szarek's prediction. When Violet turned sixteen, she ran away to marry an Italian boy, Carlo. Rose married an Irish boy, Jimmy, and Lily married a Welsh boy, David. Mary taught fifth grade in the public school, but on Saturday mornings she held Polish classes in the church. Later, Mary married the school principal, a German man named Thomas. Altogether, Leon and Anetka had sixteen grandchildren. Leon called their grandchildren a "League of Nations."

Anetka never became an American citizen, but Leon and Jozef did. Jozef attended school, though he never got past the fourth-grade primer. He participated in the 1900 and 1902 strikes. During the 1902 strike, thirteen-year-old Jozef organized a school walkout when he realized that his teacher was not a union sympathizer. "This school will never amount to anything unless it's organized," he told the children. Jozef was suspended, and that ended his school days. He left Lattimer and worked for the railroad, traveling across the country. When the United States entered World War I, Jozef enlisted. In 1918, he was killed in France during the battle of the Meuse-Argonne. He was twenty-nine.

Lidia gave birth to a baby boy three weeks after Jerzy was buried. After the christening. Lidia and her children returned to Poland, where she was reunited with her parents.

Anetka never saw Babcia again, but she continued writing to her, and Anetka and Stefania exchanged letters for the rest of their lives. Once Anetka and Leon were married, Anetka thought that over time, Leon's kisses would become respectable, plain and simple, the way Stanley's had been. She was wrong. Throughout their marriage, Leon's kisses continued to stick her feet to the floor. When she and Leon celebrated their sixty-eighth wedding anniversary, someone asked her the secret to a successful marriage. Anetka replied, "To know love in your life, you must know love in your heart." In 1965, Anetka suffered a stroke and died. A heartbroken Leon passed away the next day.

LIFE IN AMERICA
IN 1896

HISTORICAL NOTE

Although Anetka Kaminska and her family and friends are fictional characters, the anthracite coal mine patch village of Lattimer, Pennsylvania and the historical action leading to the 1897 Lattimer Massacre are real. Some day-to-day events have been reconstructed through research of contemporary newspapers, magazines, books, maps, city directories, oral histories, photographs, as well as books and articles published on the massacre in recent years. Other day-to-day events are the product of imagination.

Life for immigrants has never been easy, yet despite the hardships, Polish Americans are proud of their accomplishments as well as their sacrifices. Anetka and her family and friends were called "Slavs" by the English-speaking and American-born people in the anthracite coal region. The Slavs were from countries in eastern Europe and the Balkans. They were Poles, Ukrainians, Czechs, Slovaks, Serbians, Croatians, and several other nationalities. Large numbers of non-Slavic people such as Lithuanians, Hungarians, and Italians also settled in the anthracite region of Pennsylvania. No matter what country the immigrants came from, the English-speaking and American-born citizens lumped them together and called them "foreigners."

Rural Poland was a turbulent place during the nineteenth century. During this time, Poland was divided and ruled by three countries: Russia, Germany, and Austria. Like Tata, many Poles were peasant farmers who could no longer make a living from the land. They immigrated to the United States, looking for work and a way to feed their families. Many Poles fled their villages to escape the powerful feudal overlord system, the czarist regime, conscription in the czar's army, and ethnic, political, and religious persecution. "Whether we rot here or there," said one Polish peasant who immigrated to the United States, "it's all the same to us. At any rate, we want to try our luck." For those who loved their homeland, immigration became a necessary sacrifice to preserve their Polish culture.

Poles already in America wrote letters to family and friends, encouraging them to emigrate. "People would write friends and family still living in the old country and tell them that jobs were to be had in the mines," said George Barron, a former mine worker. "These men would line up a job for their friends and find them a place to board. . . . In about a month, the new immigrant would arrive in New York and come straight [to the mine]. He would arrive with nothing but the clothes on his back."

Other Poles were recruited by American industries

and agents, such as Mr. Bogdan, who worked for shipping and railroad lines. The German, Russian, and Austrian governments even encouraged the Poles to emigrate; shipping agents had offices in towns and villages throughout eastern Europe. Once in America, the shipping agents arranged for railroad transportation to one of the anthracite collieries, where housing and work awaited them. As soon as they arrived at their destination, the new mine workers were assigned to a boardinghouse. Often as many as thirty men crowded into a four-room house. In worse cases, a dozen men might room together in a one-room cellar. (Company housing was reserved for married men and their families.)

The new mine workers bought their mining supplies "on the book" at the company store, and the next day they marched off to work. Each new miner carried a lunch pail and wore a new pair of coveralls, a miner's hat fitted with a carbide lamp, a pick, and a shovel. On payday, their board and company store purchases were deducted from their wages. In many cases, they also owed money to the shipping agent, who usually "bought" their jobs for them from a mine foreman. The fee might be as much as the first month's wages. Even so, wages were considered high compared with other industries, and work was plentiful compared with opportunities in their homelands.

By 1900, nearly thirty-eight thousand Poles had settled in the anthracite coal region of Pennsylvania. Hardworking and eager to prove themselves, Polish men often accepted the worst and most dangerous mine jobs for the least pay. Devoted to family and friends, they were frequently the first to volunteer for risky rescue operations after an explosion or other mine disaster. Many times, their bravery cost them their lives or resulted in injury. During a twenty-year period, more Poles were killed in the anthracite mines than any other nationality. Yet Poles found little sympathy among many Americans, who didn't understand their Old World language, habits, and customs. Some Americans feared that these foreigners were stealing their jobs. "They are eager to work for wages on which an Englishman would starve," said Henry Edward Rood, a magazine reporter for *Century Illustrated Monthly Magazine.* Repeated instances of prejudice and discrimination fueled tensions between the Americans and the immigrants.

Like the men, Polish women were valued for their work habits, and a hardworking young woman from the "old country" was highly valued as a bride. Courtship was an important and serious business, especially in the anthracite region, where eligible women were scarce. Like Tata, some fathers realized that a marriageable daughter was a financial asset, especially when a bridegroom offered to pay for her passage from the old country. A father sought a son-in-law who was a hard worker and didn't squander his money.

Such matchmaking resulted in arranged marriages for

many women, some as young as Anetka. Once married, the couple moved into a company shanty and often took in boarders. Each morning, the wife stoked the coal stove, cooked breakfast for her family and boarders, and packed lunches. After the men left for work, she scavenged coal at the culm bank, chopped wood, hauled water for cooking and cleaning, baked bread, tended the garden and live-stock, picked berries and mushrooms to sell and to can, shopped for food and products she could not grow or make herself, cooked dinner, prepared the bathwater for the men, scrubbed their backs, and mended and sewed.

Large families were common, usually ranging from five to ten children, and babies were delivered at home by a midwife. Infant mortality rates were high: In some min-ing towns, 40 percent of the children died before reaching maturity. Some died at birth; others died from diseases such as measles, cholera, or typhoid. A woman rested for a day or two after childbirth, then returned to her chores. By the time a coal miner's wife was twenty, she often looked much older, because of the hardship of housework and childbirth. When a woman was widowed, her family and friends turned to matchmaking again.

Eager to preserve their heritage, many immigrant par-ents sent their children to parochial school to learn their national history, language, and religious traditions as well as American subjects. For many children, a fourth-grade education was considered adequate. By the time they were ten years old, many boys and girls quit school to work. Boys worked at the mines; girls worked in factories and mills or were hired out as domestic help. Some girls quit school to help their own mothers or to raise younger brothers and sisters when their mothers died.

Although most immigrants saw America as a land of opportunity, some immigrants never intended to stay. They intended to return home to buy a farm or to pay debts once they saved enough money. Those who did stay became naturalized citizens as soon as possible. They understood the privilege of voting for their government, a right they didn't have in the old country. It upset some Americans that "foreigners" were earning the right to vote. "Each of these foreign miners insists on voting as soon as possible," said Henry Edward Rood. "[They insist] that every good foreigner should obtain his 'papers' as soon as possible and vote at the coming election, lest the 'white men' [English-speaking, American-born men] throw too many votes into the ballotbox and pass a law to drive them out of the country."

Although several strikes occurred in the anthracite region from 1865 to 1897, each strike ended with no real gains. It was difficult to organize people who spoke so many different languages. (At least twenty-six languages were spoken in the anthracite region.) When the Lattimer massacre occurred on September 10, 1897, it was the worst American labor disaster in history. Because some of the wounded were tended at home, there are no exact casualty numbers. At least nineteen strikers died, and thirty-two were wounded.

After the shooting, three thousand men marched to Gomer Jones's house in Audenreid. They broke down doors and smashed windows. They ransacked the house, destroying everything in sight. They also stole more than two hundred dollars' worth of silverware. The value of the silverware was more than most mine workers made in a year.

When the state militia was called in, some mine workers returned to work on September 13. Angry at the men for giving up, the women retaliated. A Slavic woman named "Big Mary" Septak organized an army of 150 women and girls. They armed themselves with rolling pins, pokers, and clubs and attacked the Lattimer men. A squad of militia cavalry chased them away. The next day, the women marched ten miles and attacked the workers at a McAdoo colliery. By September 16, the women raided five more collieries. Unaccustomed to fighting women, the militia men didn't know what to do. They said the women were much harder to handle than men. The newspapers called Big Mary and her army "amazons."

On September 17, when the women struck again at McAdoo, they were stopped by mounted troopers. Undaunted, the women climbed a culm bank and threw coal at them. After the troopers left, the women attacked two more collieries. On September 18, Big Mary and her army tried to keep several hundred Lattimer men from returning to work. The militia fixed bayonets and formed a skirmish line. This didn't stop Big Mary. Armed with a wooden sword, she led a charge right up to the line. But the women's efforts weren't enough to keep the men from working. By September 28, the mines were running again.

Later that fall, Sheriff James Martin and his deputies went on trial. Their attorney called the four hundred striking workers a "barbarian horde" who didn't believe in government and law. He argued that the sheriff and his men shot the strikers in order to prevent a riot from breaking out in the region between the immigrants and native-born Americans. The jury agreed. They returned a verdict of not guilty.

Shocked by the verdict, the anthracite mine workers realized that they had to unite against the powerful coal company bosses and owners. To do so, they needed the United Mine Workers union. It took several major strikes for the miners to win better working and living conditions, and women and children played active roles in each strike. The bloodshed at Lattimer and the heroic efforts of the Poles and other immigrants made the changes possible.

Throughout the nineteenth century, various governments oppressed the Poles, even banning their language. The preservation of the Polish language and traditions is a testament to the pride, strength, and determination of the Polish people. Here are some common Polish names and terms.

Babcia (BOB-cha) — *Grandmother*

Dziadek (JAW-deck) — *Grandfather*

Mamusia (maw-MOO-shaw) — *Mother*

Tata (TAH-ta) — *Father*

Masz hart ducha (mawsh hart DOO-haw) — *You have a spirited heart*

Nazywam sie (nah-ZY-vahm shen) — *My name is*

Gospoda (gos-POH-da) — *a gathering place for men where they often drink*

Dzien dobry (jane DOH-bry) — *Good day* or *Hello*

Droga Swieta Anno! (DROH-ga SHVYEN-tah AWN-noh) — *Dear Saint Ann!*

Biedna sierota Anetka! (BYED-nah she-RO-tah aw-NET-kah) — *Poor motherless Anetka!*

Glupi kogut! (GWOO-pee KOH-goot) — *Stupid rooster!*

O, on jest trudny! (oh ohn jest TROODY-ny) — *Oh, he is impossible*

Moje dzieci! (MO-yeh JEH-chee) — *My children!*

Uparty brat (oo-PAR-tyh braht) — *Stubborn brother*

Oberek (o-BER-rek) — *a popular Polish dance*

Co dzien (tso-jane) — *Every day*

Co za piekny poranek (tso zah PYENK-nyh poh-RAH-neck) — *A beautiful morning*

Wigilia (vee-GEEL-yah) — *Holy Supper on Christmas Eve*

Pasterka (poss-TERK-kah) — *Shepherd's watch*

Kocham cie (KO-hahm chen) — *I love you*

Leniwa zona (LEH-nyivah ZHO-nah) — *Lazy wife*

Moj Boze! (mooy BO-zhe) — *an appeal to God*

Przeprasam (pshe-PRAH-shawm) — *I'm sorry* or *Excuse me*

Pomoz mi (PO-moozh mee) — *Help me*

Nie chce (nye htsen) — *I don't want it.*

Przestan! (PSHE-stein) — *Stop it!*

Milo mi (ME-woh mee) — *It's pleasant* or *It's nice*

O jej! (oh yey!) — *Oh, my!*

O nie! (oh nyeh!) — *Oh, no!*

Psia Krew! (Pshaw kref) — *Dog's blood!*

At the end of the nineteenth century, immigrants from all over the world came to America with the hopes of finding better work and an easier life. Many of them were fleeing oppressive leaders and discrimination in Eastern Europe. After their long trip across the Atlantic, the Statue of Liberty was a welcome sight. It symbolized the freedom they believed they would enjoy in this new land.

Many Polish immigrants settled in the anthracite region of Pennsylvania where life was hard. Like their thatch-roofed houses in Poland, above, their accommodations here were quite basic.

Many young girls joined family members in America. Some could afford their passage only because men they did not know paid for their tickets in exchange for their hands in marriage. Most were put directly to work as wives and homemakers upon their arrival. While the traditional Polish wedding clothes can be quite elaborate, peasant brides often wore something like the dress shown here.

*As money and resources were scarce, a coal-mining household was crowded.
Sometimes as many as fourteen people shared a one-room house.*

The wife of a coal miner had a long and grueling workday. Among her many tasks were cooking for her household, cleaning the house, and tending to her children. Here, women wait their turn to fill their buckets at a water pump that served twenty-five families.

From the youngest boys to the oldest men, the miners formed a group made up of many different nationalities and cultures. At least 26 languages were spoken in the anthracite region. Even though the Americans in the mining industry had only been citizens for a few generations themselves, they considered the immigrant miners to be outsiders and oftentimes treated them accordingly.

The sound of the breaker whistle woke the whole town every morning before dawn. The breaker is the tall building that presided over the mine where coal was broken and sorted, usually by the youngest boys. This photograph shows one of the Lattimer breakers.

Inside the breaker, the boys seated themselves at the bottom of the iron chutes where they weeded out the culm, or refuse, from the coal that slid down the chutes from the top of the breaker. Because the boys were not allowed to wear gloves, the sharp edges of the coal cut their fingers, and their hands would dry out, crack, and bleed. The average breaker boy earned a mere 70 cents a day.

At the culm pile, women and girls foraged coal for their home stoves.

Down in the mines, a boy opens the door for a mine car. He must be on hand from when the first trip of cars enters in the morning until the last comes out at night. For ten hours each day, his duty is to open and shut the door which controls and regulates the ventilation of the mine. He is alone in the darkness and silence all day.

Mining was a difficult and dangerous job. Some tunnels were so narrow that miners crawled on their hands and knees, or even on their bellies in order to get to the coal. All too often, miners died underground from collapsing mines, suffocation, or explosions. Miners' wives waited anxiously every day for their husbands and sons to arrive home safely. Here, the "Black Maria" unloads another victim.

Due to unfair treatment by the coal bosses, some coal miners organized a strike. This is a picture of those strikers on their way to Lattimer on September 10, 1897. Although they were unarmed and marching peacefully, police opened fire on the group. At the end of the Lattimer Massacre, 19 lay dead, and many others were injured. Eventually, the miners formed one union, hoping that if they worked together, their demands for reform would be met.

Potato Dumplings
(Kartoflane Kluski)

2 cups hot mashed potatoes

1/3 cup fine dry bread crumbs

2 egg yolks

3/4 teaspoon salt

1/4 teaspoon pepper

1/3 cup flour

2 egg whites, beaten until stiff but not dry

1. Mix all ingredients in a large bowl in the order given.

2. Place mixture on floured board. Roll to pencil thickness. Cut into two- or three-inch pieces.

3. Drop into boiling salted water. Cook until dumplings float to the top. Remove and drain.

4. Saute 1/2 cup onions in two tablespoons butter.

5. Add dumplings to the onions and fry until heated through and golden brown.

Potatoes were a staple food for many Polish families.

DOWN IN A COAL MINE

Simply -- Not too slow (♩ = 56)

1. I am a jo - vi - al col - lier lad, and blithe as blithe can be,_____ For let the times be good or bad they're all the same to me;_____ 'Tis lit - tle of the world I know and care less for its ways,_____ For where the dog star nev - er glows I wear a - way my days._____

2. My hands are horn - y, hard and black from work - ing in the vein,_____ And like the clothes up - on my back my speech is rough and plain;_____ Well, if I stum - ble with my tongue I've one ex - cuse to say,_____ 'Tis not the col - lier's heart that's wrong, 'tis the head that goes a - stray._____

CHORUS

Down in__ a coal mine, un-der-neath the ground,

Where a gleam of sun - shine nev - er can be found;___

Dig - ging dusk - y dia - monds all__ the sea - son round,___

rit

Down in__ a coal mine, un-der-neath the ground.___

3. At every shift, be it soon or late,
   I haste my bread to earn,
   And anxiously my kindred wait
   and watch for my return;
   For death that levels all alike,
   whate'er their rank may be,
   Amid the fire and damp may
   strike and fling his darts at me.

4. How little do the great ones care
   who sit at home secure,
   What hidden dangers colliers
   dare, what hardships they endure;
   The very fires their mansions boast,
   to cheer themselves and wives,
   Mayhap were kindled at the cost
   of jovial colliers' lives.

5. Then cheer up, lads, and make ye much of every joy ye can;
   But let your mirth be always such as best becomes a man;
   However fortune turns about well still be jovial souls,
   For what would America be without the lads that look for coals.

This telling song has become a part of the culture and tradition of the people in the Pennsylvania anthracite region. It was written in 1872.

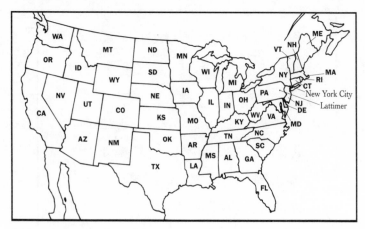

This modern map shows the approximate locations of New York City, New York, and Lattimer, Pennsylvania.

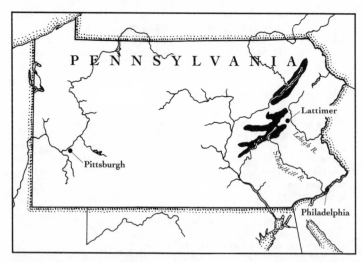

This detail of the Pennsylvania anthracite region shows where coal and coal-mining towns like Lattimer are located. Coal has long been Pennsylvania's most important mineral resource.

ABOUT THE AUTHOR

About writing *A Coal Miner's Bride*, SUSAN CAMP-BELL BARTOLETTI says, "I owe this book to strong women. I am not Polish, but when I first started to think about Anetka and her qualities and traits, I thought about the strong women in my family: my grandmother who ran a boardinghouse; my mother who was widowed at twenty-three and left with two small children; my husband's grandmother who was married at thirteen to a coal miner and had her first baby at fourteen; my mother-in-law who knows the old ways; and my daughter who is learning the ways of her mother and grandmothers while still forging her own path.

"As I researched the background for Anetka's life, I grew deeply interested in Polish culture, and I fell in love with the language, the history, and the traditions. I talked to women who came from Poland or whose mothers or grandmothers came from Poland. I heard the women's stories and personal memories about arranged marriages, daily village life, births and deaths of children, immigration to the United States, the hardships of adjusting to a new country, and the hardships of trying to preserve a culture.

"I also considered the strong women in immigrant and labor history. In my readings, I was particularly taken with the real-life character of "Big Mary" Septak (Maria Septakova), and I modeled the fictional character of Mrs. Szarek after her. Not much is written about Big Mary, but we know that she ran a Lattimer boardinghouse for Slavic immigrants. Several sources describe her as an outspoken, powerfully built woman who ordered her boarders around as if they were children.

"Big Mary was considered the most troublesome of all the foreigners after the Lattimer massacre, especially when she led an army of women to attack the troops and the men who returned to work. Big Mary valued endurance and strength, and she had contempt for American women, who, in her opinion, were weak and incapable of working in the fields because the food they ate was too sweet. According to Big Mary, the American women would be stronger if they ate more sour soup and sour cabbage.

"Was Big Mary right? Not necessarily. Strong women are found across all cultures. But her perception fascinated me, and as writers know, truth isn't found in facts, but in the way we think about facts. In order to write Anetka's story, I researched for several months, gathering, evaluating, and interpreting as many facts as I could. Then I considered those facts through the minds, perceptions, and experiences of my characters. Only then could I make Anetka's story as true as possible."

Susan Campbell Bartoletti taught eighth grade for eighteen years before becoming a full-time writer. Her nonfiction photo-essay, *Growing Up in Coal Country*, won the Jane Addams Children's Book Award and the SCBWI Golden Kite Nonfiction Honor Award, and was also named an ALA Notable Book, a YALSA Best Book for Young Adults, and a *Booklist* Editor's Choice Book, among its many other distinctions. Ms. Bartoletti lives in Pennsylvania with her family.

ACKNOWLEDGMENTS

I'm deeply grateful to the following people for their expertise: Chester Kulesa, curator, Anthracite Heritage Museum; Helen Dende, Elaine Slivinski Lisandrelli, Barbara Jablonski, Stella Ziec Kaminski, Diane Kaminski, and Rosetta Kwolek Cancelleri for their knowledge of Poland and its culture; Rick Myers, for his knowledge of bees; Bambi Lobdell, for her knowledge of herbs and soapmaking; Thom Brucie, for his knowledge of the Roman Catholic church and its traditions; Tracy Mack, for believing in Anetka; my writers' group; and my family, who eat take-out when I'm on deadline. Additional resources include oral histories and transcripts located at the Bureau of Archives and History at the Pennsylvania Historical and Museum Commission, Harrisburg, and at Eckley Miners' Village, Weatherly, Pennsylvania; contemporary newspapers, magazines, and local history resources located at the Hazleton Public Library, Hazleton, Pennsylvania, and at the Scranton Public Library, Scranton, Pennsylvania; Tina at Majestic Mountain Sage at www.the-sage.com, and Belinda at tdale.demon.co.uk.

Grateful acknowledgment is made for permission to reprint the following:

Cover Portrait: Sergei Mikhailovich Prokudin-Gorskii, Library of Congress.

Cover Background: Paul Thomas Studio, Shamokin, Pennsylvania.

Page 204 (top): Wood engraving, *Frank Leslie's Illustrated Newspaper,* July 2, 1887.

Page 204 (bottom): Thatch-roofed house in Polish countryside, Obrebski Collection, Special Collection and Archives, W.E.B. DuBois Library, University of Massachusetts/Amherst.

Page 205: Girl in wedding garb, The Kosciusko Foundation, Inc. An American Center for Polish Culture Archive.

Page 206: A Room Where Fourteen Live, *Century Illustrated Monthly Magazine,* vol. 55, 1898. pg. 824.

Page 207 (top): Economy in a mining town, Pennsylvania Historical and Museum Commission, Anthracite Museum Complex, Scranton, Pennsylvania.

Page 207 (bottom): Pennsylvania coal mine, Library of Congress, LC-USZ62-27919

Page 208 (top): Lattimer Braker (sic), Hazleton, PA. Postcard Collection of Charles Kumpas, Clarks Summit.

Page 208 (bottom): Boys at chutes, Wyoming Historical and Geological Society, Wilkes-Barre, Pennsylvania.

Page 209 (top): Pickers at culm banks, ibid.

Page 209 (bottom): Door opener, Lewis Hine Collection, Library of Congress, LC-USZ62-23745.

Page 210 (top): Black Maria, Wyoming Historical and Geological Society, Wilkes-Barre, Pennsylvania.

Page 210 (bottom): Strikers en route to Lattimer, MG-273, Charles H. Burg Collection, Pennsylvania State Archives.

Page 212–213: "Down in a Coal Mine." *The Miner Sings: A Collection of Folk Songs and Ballads of the Anthracite Miner.* Transcribed and arranged by Melvin Le Mon. J. Fischer & Bro. New York. 1872.

Page 214: Maps by Heather Saunders.

For Elaine, who has hart ducha

-:::--:::--:::-

While the events described and some of the characters
in this book may be based on actual historical events
and real people, Anetka Kaminska is a fictional character,
created by the author, and her diary and its epilogue
are works of fiction.

Library of Congress Cataloging-in-Publication Data
Bartoletti, Susan Campbell.
A coal miner's bride: the diary of Anetka Kaminska
Lattimer, Pennsylvania, 1896
by Susan Campbell Bartoletti
p. cm.
Summary: A diary account of thirteen-year-old Anetka, life in Poland
in 1896, immigration to America, marriage to a coal miner, widowhood,
and happiness in finally finding her true love.
ISBN 0-439-05386-2 (hardcover : alk. paper)
[1. Immigrants — Fiction.   2. Polish Americans — Fiction.
3. Coal Miners — Fiction.   4. Diaries — Fiction.]   I. Title.   II. Series.
PZ7.B2844Co   2000
[Fic] — dc21   99-29864
CIP AC

10 9 8 7 6 5 4 3   0/0 01 02 03 04 05

The display type was set in Aquitain Initials.
The text type was set in Cochin.
Book design by Elizabeth B. Parisi
Photo research by Susan Campbell Bartoletti, Zoe Moffitt, and Jai Imbrey

Printed in the U.S.A. 23
First printing, July 2000

-:::--:::--:::-